More Praise for *H*

T0304463

"Exquisite prose . . . *Hot Milk* is perfect so mesmerising that reading it is to be end is like finding a piece of glass on th by the sea, that can be held up and looked into like a glass-eye and kept, in secret, to be looked at again and again." —Suzanne Joinson, *The Independent*

"A captivating demonstration of why Levy is one of the few necessary novelists writing in Britain today. This is the poetry and playfulness of her prose . . . More important, Levy grapples with and presents the complex psychology and multiple facets of her female characters like few others, which makes the recent reappraisal of her life's work all the more welcome." —Liam Hoare, *Forward*

"Great lush writing [and] luxuriation in place. No writer infuses the landscape, urban or rural, with as much meaning and monstrosity as Levy . . . Unmissable." —Eimear McBride, *New Statesman*

"Acutely relevant . . . A triumph of technically adroit storytelling. Levy's elegant and poised prose has the rare quality of being simultaneously expansive and succinct . . . A breath of fresh air." —*The Literary Review*

"A beguiling tale of myths and identity . . . Provocative . . . The difficult, ambivalent, precious mother-daughter relationship forms the core of this beautiful, clever novel." —Michèle Roberts, *The Independent*

"The novel [has an] eerie atmosphere and sibylline turns of phrase . . . Its moody spell and haunted imagery pull you in." —Sam Sacks, *The Wall Street Journal*

"Levy's language is precise . . . Her style . . . yield[s] a larger pattern: a commentary on debt and personal responsibility, family ties and independence." —Jamie Fisher, *The Washington Post*

"Among the questions posed in this heady new novel: Is Sofia's mother, Rose, sick or a hypochondriac who's feverish for attention? And more important, can the frustrated Sofia break the chains of familial devotion and live for herself?" —O, *The Oprah Magazine*

"A complicated, gorgeous work." —Steph Opitz, *Marie Claire*

"Deborah Levy's intoxicating and beautifully crafted novel, a worthy finalist for the Man Booker Prize, digs deep in its exploration of female sexuality, strained family bonds and hypochondria." —Malcolm Forbes, *Minneapolis Star Tribune*

"Deborah Levy conveys an atmosphere of out-of-kilter surreality without ever violating the rules of realism. There's no magic here, aside from the supernatural powers of peculiar prose." —Lionel Shriver, *Financial Times*

"Economical, fluid, evocative of sex and mythology . . . Young Sofia . . . drop[s] beautiful bombs of truth." —*New York* magazine's *Vulture* blog

"*Hot Milk*, Deborah Levy's intensely interior but highly charged new novel about family, hypochondria, Spain, Greece, and all kinds of sex." —*New York* magazine's Approval Matrix

"A singular read . . . Levy has crafted a great character in Sofia, and witnessing a pivotal point in her life is a pleasure." —*Publishers Weekly* (starred and boxed review)

"Scintillating, provocative . . . Levy combines intellect and empathy to impressively modern effect." —*Kirkus Reviews* (starred review)

"The author of the elusive, powerful novel *Swimming Home* has another tale of family dysfunction. In the unforgiving heat of southern Spain, wayward anthropologist Sofia Papastergiadis delivers her mother into the hands of an eccentric doctor whom they hope can diagnose the mysterious illness that has taken over her body." —Elle.com

"Haunting . . . Unforgettable and complex." —Bethanne Patrick, LitHub

"A fascinating book about sexuality, anger, medicine, and the drive to stay alive, *Hot Milk* is a unique novel that reads like a lucid dream." —*Bustle*

"Levy's language is so precise, so dreamlike, that reading it takes the reader into some heightened, impossible state." —*Vox*

"A superbly crafted novel that is an inherently fascinating and consistently compelling read from beginning to end, *Hot Milk* clearly reveals author Deborah Levy as an exceptionally gifted storyteller." —*Midwest Book Review*

"Mesmerizing . . . Evocative and complex." —*Booklist*

"The Man Booker short-listed Levy . . . draws in readers with beautiful language and unexpected moments of humor and shock." —*Library Journal*

"Family dynamics, long-kept secrets and a mother-daughter relationship drive this novel set against the sweltering landscape of southern Spain. But don't be mistaken into thinking this slim book is a lightweight 'beach read.' Levy's lean, poetic style (last seen in her Booker shortlisted *Swimming Home*) delivers considerable heft." —BookBrowse

"A terrific tale of mothers and daughters and fathers and daughters and confusion and old age, sickness, woe . . . and finding love tucked away in strange places." —*RALPH* magazine

"Dazzling and, at times, deeply disturbing, *Hot Milk* is a mystery meets introspective coming-of-age novel. It's unnerving—and that's a good thing." —*Refinery29*

"Levy's reputation as a singularly talented writer is on display throughout this novel, and this is most obvious at the basic level of the sentence. Her prose is lean and taut, poetic and rich with symbolism; each sentence shaped with care with nary a redundant word." —*PopMatters*

"*Hot Milk* is a purposeful work of how someone might find sustenance." —*Daily Kos*

"A fraught, intense bond between mother and daughter is poetically rendered in *Hot Milk*, Deborah Levy's follow-up to the 2012 Man Booker short-listed *Swimming Home*." —*San Diego Magazine*

"*Hot Milk* tells the story of mother and daughter as they travel to Spain to seek out the expertise of a famous consultant. As the treatment continues, the symptoms become ever more strange and the book even harder to put down." —*HelloGiggles*

"What can be more fraught than a mother/daughter relationship? . . . Deborah Levy takes this to the extreme in her sizzling novel, *Hot Milk*." —*CounterPunch*

HOT MILK

HOT MILK

Deborah Levy

BLOOMSBURY

NEW YORK · LONDON · OXFORD · NEW DELHI · SYDNEY

Bloomsbury USA
An imprint of Bloomsbury Publishing Plc

1385 Broadway   50 Bedford Square
New York   London
NY 10018   WC1B 3DP
USA   UK

www.bloomsbury.com

BLOOMSBURY and the Diana logo are trademarks of Bloomsbury Publishing Plc

First published by Hamish Hamilton 2016
First U.S. edition 2016
This paperback edition 2017

ISBN: HB: 978-1-62040-669-4
ePub: 978-1-62040-671-7
PB: 978-1-62040-670-0

LIBRARY OF CONGRESS CATALOGING-IN-PUBLICATION DATA

Levy, Deborah
Hot milk : a novel / Deborah Levy.
p.cm.
ISBN 978-1-62040-669-4 (hardcover) | ISBN 978-1-62040-671-7 (ebook)
Parent and adult child—Fiction. | Mothers and
daughters—Fiction. | Self-realization in women—Fiction. |
Self-actualization (Psychology) in women—Fiction.
LCC PR6062.E9255 H68 2016 (print) | LCC PR6062.E9255 (ebook)
DDC 823/.914—dc23

10

Typeset by Jouve (UK), Milton Keynes
Printed and bound in the U.S.A. by Sheridan, Chelsea, Michigan.

To find out more about our authors and books visit www.bloomsbury.com. Here you
will find extracts, author interviews, details of forthcoming events, and the option to sign up for our newsletters.

Bloomsbury books may be purchased for business or promotional use.
For information on bulk purchases please contact Macmillan Corporate and
Premium Sales Department at specialmarkets@macmillan.com.

It's up to you to break the old circuits.

— Hélène Cixous, 'The Laugh of the Medusa'

2015. Almería. Southern Spain. August.

Today I dropped my laptop on the concrete floor of a bar built on the beach. It was tucked under my arm and slid out of its black rubber sheath (designed like an envelope), landing screen side down. The digital page is now shattered but at least it still works. My laptop has all my life in it and knows more about me than anyone else.

So what I am saying is that if it is broken, so am I.

My screen saver is an image of a purple night sky crowded with stars, and constellations and the Milky Way, which takes its name from the classical Latin *lactea*. My mother told me years ago that I must write Milky Way like this – γαλαξίας κύκλος – and that Aristotle gazed up at the milky circle in Chalcidice, thirty-four miles east of modern-day Thessaloniki, where my father was born. The oldest star is about 13 billion years old but the stars on my screen saver are two years old and were made in China. All this universe is now shattered.

There is nothing I can do about it. Apparently, there is a cybercafé in the next flyblown town and the man who owns it sometimes mends minor computer faults, but he'd have to send for a new screen and it will take a month to arrive. Will I still be here in a month? I don't know. It depends on my sick mother, who is sleeping under a mosquito net in the next room. She will wake up and shout, 'Get me water, Sofia,' and I will get her water and it will always be the wrong sort of water. I am not sure what water means any more but I will get her water as I understand it: from a bottle in the fridge, from a bottle that is not in the fridge, from the kettle in which the water has been boiled and left to cool. When I gaze at the star fields on my screen saver I often float out of time in the most peculiar way.

It's only 11 p.m. and I could be floating on my back in the sea look-ing up at the real night sky and the real Milky Way but I am nervous about jellyfish. Yesterday afternoon I got stung and it left a fierce purple whiplash welt on my left upper arm. I had to run across the hot sand to the injury hut at the end of the beach to get some ointment from the male student (full beard) whose job it is to sit there all day attending to tourists with stings. He told me that in Spain jellyfish are called medusas. I thought the Medusa was a Greek goddess who became a monster after being cursed and that her powerful gaze turned anyone who looked into her eyes to stone. So why would a jellyfish be named after her? He said yes, but he was guessing that the tentacles of the jellyfish resemble the hair of the Medusa, which in pictures is always a tangled mess of writhing snakes.

I had seen the cartoon Medusa image printed on the yellow danger flag outside the injury hut. She has tusks for teeth and crazy eyes.

'When the Medusa flag is flying it is best not to swim. Really it is at your own discretion.'

He dabbed the sting with cotton wool which he had soaked in heated-up seawater and then asked me to sign a form that looked like a petition. It was a list of all the people on the beach who had been stung that day. The form asked me for my name, age, occupation and country of origin. That's a lot of information to think about when your arm is blistered and burning. He explained he was required to ask me to fill it in to keep the injury hut open in the Spanish recession. If tourists did not have cause to use this service he would be out of a job, so he was obviously pleased about the medusas. They put bread in his mouth and petrol in his moped.

Peering at the form, I could see that the age of the people on the beach stung by medusas ranged from seven to seventy-four, and they mostly came from all over Spain but there were a few tourists from the UK and someone from Trieste. I have always wanted to go to Trieste because it sounds like tristesse, which is a light-hearted word, even though in French it means sadness. In Spanish it is tristeza, which is heavier than French sadness, more of a groan than a whisper.

I hadn't seen any jellyfish while I was swimming but the student explained that their tentacles are very long so they can sting at a distance. His forefinger was sticky with the ointment he was now rubbing into my arm. He seemed well informed about jellyfish. The medusas are transparent because they are 95 per cent water, so they camouflage easily. Also, one of the reasons there are so many of them in the oceans of the world is because of over-fishing. The main thing was to make sure I didn't rub or scratch the welts. There might still be jellyfish cells on my arm and rubbing the sting encourages them to release more venom, but his special ointment would deactivate the stinging cells. As he talked I could see his soft, pink lips pulsing like a medusa in the middle of his beard. He handed me a pencil stub and asked me to please fill in the form.

Name: Sofia Papastergiadis
Age: 25
Country of origin: UK
Occupation:

The jellyfish don't care about my occupation, so what is the point? It is a sore point, more painful than my sting and more of a problem than my surname which no one can say or spell. I told him I have a degree in anthropology but for the time being I work in a café in West London – it's called the Coffee House and it's got free Wi-Fi and renovated church pews. We roast our own beans and make three types of artisan espresso . . . so I don't know what to put under 'Occupation'.

3

The student tugged at his beard. 'So do you anthropologists study primitive people?'

'Yes, but the only primitive person I have ever studied is myself.'

I suddenly felt homesick for Britain's gentle, damp parks. I wanted to stretch my primitive body flat out on green grass where there were no jellyfish floating between the blades. There is no green grass in Almería except on the golf courses. The dusty, barren hills are so parched they used to film Spaghetti Westerns here – one even starred Clint Eastwood. Real cowboys must have had cracked lips all the time because my lips have started to split from the sun and I put lipsalve on them every day. Perhaps the cowboys used animal fat? Did they gaze out at the infinite sky and miss the absence of kisses and caresses? And did their own troubles disappear in the mystery of space like they sometimes do when I gaze at the galaxies on my shattered screen saver?

The student seemed quite knowledgeable about anthropology as well as jellyfish. He wants to give me an idea for 'an original field study' while I am in Spain. 'Have you seen the white plastic structures that cover all the land in Almería?'

I *had* seen the ghostly white plastic. It stretches as far as the eye can see across the plains and valleys.

'They are greenhouses,' he said. 'The temperature inside these farms in the desert can rise to forty-five degrees. They employ illegal immigrants to pick the tomatoes and peppers for the supermarkets, but it's more or less slavery.'

I thought so. Anything covered is always interesting. There is never nothing beneath something that is covered. As a child, I used to cover my face with my hands so that no one would know I was there. And then I discovered that covering my face made me more visible because everyone was curious to see what it was I wanted to hide in the first place.

He looked at my surname on the form and then at the thumb on his left hand, which he started to bend, as if he were checking the joint was still working.

'You are Greek, aren't you?'

His attention is so unfocused it's unsettling. He never actually looks at me directly. I recite the usual: my father is Greek, my mother is English, I was born in Britain.

'Greece is a smaller country than Spain, but it can't pay its bills. The dream is over.'

I asked him if he was referring to the economy. He said yes, he was studying for a master's degree at the School of Philosophy at Granada University but he considered himself lucky to have a summer job on the beach at the injury hut. If the Coffee House was still hiring when he graduated, he would head for London. He didn't know why he had said the dream was over because he didn't believe it. He had probably read it somewhere and it stuck with him. But it wasn't his own opinion, a phrase like 'the dream is over.' For a start, who is the dreamer? The only other public dream he could remember was from Martin Luther King's speech 'I had a dream . . .', but the phrase about the dream being over implied that something had started and had now ended. It was up to the dreamer to say it was over, no one else could say it on their behalf.

And then he spoke a whole sentence to me in Greek and seemed surprised when I told him that I do not speak Greek.

It is a constant embarrassment to have a surname like Papastergiadis and not speak the language of my father.

'My mother is English.'

'Yes,' he said in his perfect English. 'I have only been to Skiathos in Greece once but I managed to pick up a few phrases.'

It was as if he was mildly insulting me for not being Greek enough. My father left my mother when I was five and she is English and mostly speaks to me in English. What did it have to do with him? And anyway the jellyfish sting was what he was supposed to be concerned about.

'I have seen you in the plaza with your mother.'

'Yes.'

'She has difficulty walking?'

'Sometimes Rose can walk, sometimes she can't.'

'Your mother's name is Rose?'

'Yes.'

'You call her by her name?'

'Yes.'

'You don't say Mama?'

'No.'

The hum of the little fridge standing in the corner of the injury hut was like something dead and cold but with a pulse. I wondered if there were bottles of water inside it. *Agua con gas*, *agua sin gas*. I am always thinking of ways to make water more right than wrong for my mother.

The student looked at his watch. 'The rule for anyone who has been stung is they have to stay here for five minutes. It's so I can check you don't have a heart attack or another reaction.'

He pointed again to 'Occupation' on the form, which I had left blank.

It might have been the pain of the sting, but I found myself telling him about my pathetic miniature life. 'I don't so much have an occupation as a preoccupation, which is my mother, Rose.'

He trailed his fingers down his shins while I spoke.

'We are here in Spain to visit the Gómez Clinic to find out what is actually wrong with her legs. Our first appointment is in three days' time.'

'Your mother has limb paralysis?'

'We don't know. It's a mystery. It's been going on for a while.'

He started to unwrap a lump of white bread covered in cling film. I thought it might be part two of the jellyfish-sting cure but it turned out to be a peanut-butter sandwich, which he said was his favourite lunch. He took a small bite and his black, glossy beard moved around while he chewed. Apparently, he knows about the Gómez Clinic. It is highly thought of and he also knows the woman who has rented us the small, rectangular apartment on the beach. We chose it because it has no stairs. Everything is on one floor, the two bedrooms are next to each other, just off the kitchen, and it is near the main square and all the cafés and the local Spar. It is also next door to the diving school, Escuela de Buceo y Náutica, a white cube on two floors with windows in the shape of portholes. The reception area is being painted at the moment. Two Mexican men set to work every morning with giant tins of white paint. A howling, lean Alsatian dog is chained all day to an iron bar on the diving-school roof terrace. He belongs to Pablo who is the director of the diving school, but Pablo is on his computer all the time playing a game called *Infinite Scuba*. The crazed dog pulls at its chains and regularly tries to leap off the roof.

'No one likes Pablo,' the student agreed. 'He's the sort of man who would pluck a chicken while it's still alive.'

'That's a good subject for an anthropological field study,' I said.

'What is?'

'Why no one likes Pablo.'

The student held up three fingers. I assumed that meant I had to stay in the injury hut for three more minutes.

In the morning, the male staff at the diving school give a tutorial to student divers about how to put on their diving suits. They are uneasy about the dog being chained up all the time, but they get on with the things they have to do. Their second task is to pour petrol through a funnel into plastic tanks and wheel them out on an electric device across the sand to load on to the boat. This is quite complicated technology compared to the Swedish masseur, Ingmar, who usually sets up his tent at the same time. Ingmar transports his massage bed on to the beach by attaching ping-pong balls to its legs and sliding it across the sand. He has complained to me personally about Pablo's dog, as if the accident of my living next door to the diving school means that I somehow co-own the miserable Alsatian. Ingmar's clients can never relax because the dog whines, howls, barks and tries to kill itself all through their aromatherapy massage.

The student in the injury hut asked me if I was still breathing.

I'm starting to think he wants to keep me here.

He held up a finger. 'You have to stay with me for one more minute, and then I will have to ask again how are you feeling.'

I want a bigger life.

What I feel most is that I am a failure but I would rather work in the Coffee House than be hired to conduct research into why customers prefer one washing machine to another. Most of the students I studied with ended up becoming corporate ethnographers. If ethnography means the writing of culture, market research is a sort of culture (where people live, the kind of environment they inhabit, how the task of washing clothes is divided between members of the community . . .) but in the end, it is about selling washing machines. I'm not sure I even want to do original fieldwork that involves lying in a hammock watching sacred buffalo grazing in the shade.

I was not joking when I said the subject of Why Everyone Hates Pablo would be a good field study.

The dream is over for me. It began when I left my lame mother alone to pick the pears from the tree in our East London garden that autumn I packed my bags for university. I won a first-class degree. It continued while I studied for my master's. It ended when she became ill and I abandoned my Ph.D. The unfinished thesis I wrote for my doctorate still lurks in a digital file behind my shattered screen saver like an unclaimed suicide.

Yes, some things are getting bigger (the lack of direction in my life), but not the right things. Biscuits in the Coffee House are getting bigger (the size of my head), receipts are getting bigger (there is so much information on a receipt, it is almost a field study in itself), also my thighs (a diet of sandwiches, pastries . . .). My bank balance is getting smaller and so are passion fruit (though pomegranates are getting bigger and so is air pollution, as is my shame at sleeping five nights of the week in the storeroom above the Coffee House). Most nights in London I collapse on the childish single bed in a stupor. I never have an excuse for being late for work. The worst part of my job is the customers who ask me to sort out their traveller's wireless mice and charging devices. They are on their way to somewhere else while I collect their cups and write labels for the cheesecake.

I stamped my feet to distract myself from the throbbing pain in my arm. And then I noticed that the halter-neck strap of my bikini top had broken and my bare breasts were juddering up and down as I stamped about. The string must have snapped when I was swimming, which means that when I ran across the beach and into the injury hut I was topless. Perhaps that is why the student did not know where to rest his eyes through our conversation. I turned my back on him while I fiddled with the straps.

'How are you feeling?'

'I'm okay.'

'You are free to leave.'

When I turned round, his eyes flickered across my newly covered breasts.

'You haven't filled in "Occupation".'

I took the pencil and wrote WAITRESS.

My mother had instructed me to wash her yellow dress with the sunflower print on it because she will wear it to her first appointment at the Gómez Clinic. That is fine by me. I like washing clothes by hand and hanging them out to dry in the sun. The burn of the sting started to throb again, despite the ointment the student had smeared all over it. My face was burning up but I think it was because of the difficulty I'd had filling in 'Occupation' on the form. It was as if the poison from the medusa sting had in turn released some venom that was lurking inside me. On Monday, my mother will display her various symptoms to the consultant like an assortment of mysterious canapés. I will be holding the tray.

There she goes. The beautiful Greek girl is walking across the beach in her bikini. There is a shadow between her body and my own. Sometimes she drags her feet in the sand. She has no one to rub suncream on her back and say here yes no yes there.

Dr Gómez

We had begun the long journey to find a healer. The taxi driver hired to take us to the Gómez Clinic had no reason to understand how nervous we were or what was at stake.

We had begun a new chapter in the history of my mother's legs and it had taken us to the semi-desert of southern Spain.

It is not a small matter. We had to remortgage Rose's house to pay for her treatment at the Gómez Clinic. The total cost was twenty-five thousand euro, which is a substantial sum to lose, considering I have been sleuthing my mother's symptoms for as long as I can remember.

My own investigation has been in progress for about twenty of my twenty-five years. Perhaps longer. When I was four I asked her what a headache meant. She told me it was like a door slamming in her head. I have become a good mind reader, which means her head is my head. There are plenty of doors slamming all the time and I am the main witness.

If I see myself as an unwilling detective with a desire for justice, does that make her illness an unsolved crime? If so, who is the villain and who is the victim? Attempting to decipher her aches and pains, their triggers and motivations, is a good training for an anthropologist. There have been times when I thought I was on the verge of a major revelation and knew where the corpses were buried, only to be thwarted once again. Rose merely presents a new and entirely mysterious symptom for which she is prescribed new and entirely mysterious medication. The U K doctors recently prescribed anti-depressants for her feet. That's what she told me – they are for the nerve endings in her feet.

The clinic was near the town of Carboneras, which is famous for its cement factory. It would be a thirty-minute ride. My mother and I sat shivering in the back of the taxi because the air conditioner had transformed the desert heat into something more like a Russian winter. The driver told us that carboneras means coal bunkers, and the mountains had once been covered in a forest, which had been cut down for charcoal. Everything had been stripped for 'the furnace'.

I asked him if he'd mind turning down the air conditioner.

He insisted the AC was automatic and out of his control, but he could advise us on where to find beaches with clear, clean water.

'The best beach is Playa de los Muertos, which means "Beach of the Dead". It is only five kilometres south of town. You will have walk down the mountain for twenty minutes. There is no access by road.'

Rose leaned forward and tapped his shoulder. 'We are here because I have a bone disease and can't walk.' She frowned at the plastic rosary hanging from his mirror. Rose is a committed atheist, all the more so since my father had a religious conversion.

Her lips had turned blue due to the extreme weather inside the car. 'As for the "Beach of the Dead" ' – she shivered as she spoke – 'I'm not quite there yet, though I can see it would be more appealing to swim in clear water than to burn in the furnace of hell, for which all the trees in the world will have to be felled and every mountain stripped for coal.' Her Yorkshire accent had suddenly become fierce, which it always does when she's enjoying an argument.

The driver's attention was on a fly that had landed on his steering wheel. 'Perhaps you will need to book my taxi for your return journey?'

'It depends on the temperature in your automobile.' Her thin, blue lips stretched into something resembling a smile as the taxi became warmer.

We were no longer stranded in a Russian winter so much as a Swedish one.

I opened the window. The valley was covered in white plastic, just as the student in the injury hut had described. The desert farms were devouring the land like a dull, sickly skin. The hot wind blew my hair across my eyes while Rose rested her head on my shoulder, which was still smarting from the jellyfish sting. I dared not move to a less painful position because I knew she was scared and that I had to pretend not to be. She had no God to plead to for mercy or luck. It would be true to say she depended instead on human kindness and painkillers.

As the driver steered his cab into the palm-fringed grounds of the Gómez Clinic, we glimpsed the gardens that had been described in the brochure as 'a mini-oasis of great ecological importance'. Two wild pigeons lay tucked into each other under the mimosa trees.

The clinic itself was carved into the scorched mountains. Built from cream-coloured marble in the shape of a dome, it resembled a massive, upside-down cup. I had studied it on Google many times, but the digital page did not convey how calming and comforting it felt to stand next to it in real time. The entrance, in contrast, was entirely made from glass. Thorny bushes with flowering purple blooms and low, tangled, silver cacti were planted abundantly around the curve of the dome, leaving the gravel entrance clear for the taxi to park next to a small, stationary shuttle bus.

It took fourteen minutes to walk with Rose from the car to the glass doors. They seemed to anticipate our arrival, opening silently for us, as if gratifying our wish to enter without either of us having to make the request.

I gazed at the deep blue Mediterranean below the mountain and felt at peace.

When the receptionist called out for Señora Papastergiadis, I took Rose's arm and we limped together across the marble floor towards the desk. Yes, we are limping together. I am twenty-five and I am limping with my mother to keep in step with her. My legs are her legs. That is how we find a convivial pace to move forwards. It is how adults walk with young children who have graduated from crawling and how adult children walk with their parents when they need an arm to lean on. Earlier that morning, my mother had walked on her own to the local Spar to buy herself some hairpins. She had not even taken a walking stick to lean on. I no longer wanted to think about that.

The receptionist directed me to a nurse who was waiting with a wheelchair. It was a relief to pass Rose over to someone else, to walk behind the nurse as she pushed the chair and admire the way she swayed her hips as she walked at a pace, her long, shining hair tied with a white, satin ribbon. This was another style of walking, entirely free of pain, of attachment to kin, of compromise. The heels of the nurse's grey suede shoes sounded like an egg cracking as she made her way down the marble corridors. Stopping outside a door with the words Mr Gómez written in gold letters across a panel of polished wood, she knocked and waited.

Her nails were painted a deep glossy red.

We had travelled a long way from home. To be here at last in this curved corridor with its amber veins threading through the walls felt like a pilgrimage of sorts, a last chance. For years, an increasing number of medical professionals in the UK had been groping in the dark for a diagnosis, puzzled, lost, humbled, resigned. This had to be the final journey and I think my mother knew that, too. A male voice shouted something in Spanish. The nurse pushed the heavy door open and then beckoned to me to wheel Rose into the room, as if to say, *She is all yours.*

Dr Gómez. The orthopaedic consultant I had researched so thoroughly for months on end. He looked like he was in his early sixties, his hair was mostly silver but with a startling pure white streak running across the left side of his head. He wore a pinstripe suit, his hands were tanned, his eyes blue and alert.

'Thank you, Nurse Sunshine,' he said to the nurse, as if it were normal for an eminent doctor who specialized in musculoskeletal conditions to name his staff after the weather. She was still holding the door open, as if her thoughts had wandered off to roam on the Sierra Nevada.

He raised his voice and repeated in Spanish, 'Gracias, Enfermera Luz del Sol.'

This time she shut the door. I could hear the cracking sound of her heels on the floor, first at an even pace and then suddenly faster. She had started to run. The echo of her heels remained in my mind long after she had left the room.

Dr Gómez spoke English with an American accent.

'Please. How can I help you?'

Rose looked baffled. 'Well, that is exactly what I want *you* to tell *me*.'

When Dr Gómez smiled, his two front teeth were entirely covered with gold. They reminded me of the teeth on a human male skull we studied in the first year of my anthropology degree, the task being to guess his diet. The teeth were full of cavities so it was likely he had chewed on tough grain. On further scrutiny of the skull, I discovered that a small square of linen had been stuffed into the larger cavity. It had been soaked in cedar oil to ease the pain and stop infection.

Dr Gómez's tone was vaguely friendly and vaguely formal. 'I have been looking at your notes, Mrs Papastergiadis. You were a librarian for some years?'

'Yes. I retired early because of my health.'

'Did you want to stop working?'

'Yes.'

'So you did not retire because of your health?'

'It was a combination of circumstances.'

15

'I see.' He looked neither bored nor interested.

'My duties were to catalogue, index and classify the books,' she said.

He nodded and turned his gaze to his computer screen. While we waited for his attention, I looked around the consulting room. It was sparsely furnished. A basin. A bed on wheels that could be lowered or raised, a silver lamp placed near it.

A cabinet filled with leather-bound books stood behind his desk. And then I saw something looking at me. Its eyes were bright and curious. A small grey stuffed monkey was crouching in a glass box on a shelf halfway up the wall. Its eyes were fixed on its human brothers and sisters in an eternal frozen stare.

'Mrs Papastergiadis, I see that your first name is Rose.'

'Yes.'

He had pronounced Papastergiadis as easily as if he were saying Joan Smith.

'May I refer to you now as Rose?'

'Yes, you may. It is my name, after all. My daughter calls me Rose and I see no reason why you should not do the same.'

Dr Gómez smiled at me. 'You call your mother Rose?'

It was the second time I had been asked this question in three days.

'Yes,' I said quickly, as if it was of no importance. 'Can we ask how we should address you, Dr Gómez?'

'Certainly. I am a consultant, so I am Mr Gómez. But that is too formal so I will not be offended if you just refer to me as Gómez.'

'Ah. That is useful to know.' My mother lifted her arm to check that the hairpin in her chignon was still in place.

'And you are just sixty-four years old, Mrs Papastergiadis?'

Had he forgotten he'd been granted permission to call his new patient by her first name?

'Sixty-four and flagging.'

'So you were thirty-nine when you birthed your daughter?'

Rose coughed as if to clear her throat and then nodded and coughed again. Gómez started to cough too. He cleared his throat and ran his fingers through the white streak in his hair. Rose moved her right leg and then she groaned. Gómez moved his left leg and then he groaned.

I was not sure if he was mimicking her or mocking her. If they were having a conversation in groans, coughs and sighs, I wondered whether they understood each other.

'It is a pleasure to welcome you to my clinic, Rose.'

He held out his hand. My mother leaned forward as if to shake it but then suddenly decided not to. His hand was stuck in the air. Obviously, their non-verbal conversation had not elicited her trust.

'Sofia, get me a tissue,' she said.

I passed her a tissue and shook Gómez's hand on behalf of my mother. Her arm is my arm.

'And you are Ms Papastergiadis?' He emphasized the 'Ms' so it sounded like *Mizzzzz*.

'Sofia is my only daughter.'

'Do you have sons?'

'As I said, she is my only.'

'Rose.' He smiled. 'I think you are going to sneeze soon. Is there pollen in the air today? Or something?'

'Pollen?' Rose looked offended. 'We are in a desert landscape. There are no flowers as I know them.'

Gómez mimicked looking offended, too. 'Later I will take you for a tour of our gardens so you can see flowers as you do not know them. Purple sea lavender, jujube shrubs with their magnificent thorny branches, Phoenician junipers and various scrubland plants imported for your pleasure from near Tabernas.'

He walked towards her wheelchair, kneeled at her feet and stared into her eyes. She started to sneeze. 'Get me another tissue, Sofia.'

I obliged. She now had two tissues, one in each hand.

'I always get a pain in my left arm after I sneeze,' she said. 'It's a sharp, tearing pain. I have to hold my arm until the sneeze is over.'

'Where is the pain?'

'The inside of my elbow.'

'Thank you. We will conduct a full neurological examination, including a cranial-nerve examination.'

'And I have chronic knuckle pain in my left hand.'

In response, he wiggled the fingers of his left hand in the direction of the monkey, as if encouraging it to do the same.

After a while he turned to me. 'I can just see the resemblance. But you, Mizz Papastergiadis, are darker. Your skin is sallow. Your hair is nearly black. Your mother's hair is light brown. Your nose is longer than hers. Your eyes are brown. Your mother's eyes are blue, like my own eyes.'

'My father is Greek but I was born in Britain.'

I wasn't sure if having sallow skin was an insult or a compliment.

'Then you are like me,' he said. 'My father is Spanish, my mother is American. I grew up in Boston.'

'Like my laptop. It was designed in America and made in China.'

'Yes, identity is always difficult to guarantee, Mizz Papastergiadis.'

'I am from near Hull, Yorkshire,' Rose suddenly announced, as if she felt left out.

When Gómez reached for my mother's right foot, she gave it to him as if it were a gift. He started to press her toes with his thumb and forefinger, watched by myself and the monkey in the glass box. His thumb moved to her ankle. 'This bone is the talus. And before that I was pressing the phalanges. Can you feel my fingers?'

Rose shook her head. 'I feel nothing. My feet are numb.'

Gómez nodded, as if he already knew this to be true. 'How is your morale?' he asked, as if enquiring about a bone called The Morale.

'Not bad at all.'

I bent down and picked up her shoes.

'Please,' Gómez said. 'Leave them where they are.' He was now feeling the sole of my mother's right foot. 'You have an ulcer here, and here. Have you been tested for diabetes?'

18

'Oh, yes,' she said.

'It is a small area on the surface of the skin, but it is slightly infected. We must attend to this immediately.'

Rose nodded gravely, but she looked pleased. 'Diabetes,' she exclaimed. 'Perhaps that's the answer.'

He did not seem to want to continue this conversation because he stood up and walked to the basin to wash his hands. He turned towards me while he reached for a paper towel. 'You will probably be interested in the architecture of my clinic?'

I *was* interested. I told him that as far as I knew, the earliest domes had been built from mammoth tusks and bones.

'Ye-es. And your beach apartment is a rectangle. But at least it has an ocean view –'

'It's unpleasant,' Rose interrupted. 'I think of it as a rectangle built on noise. It has a concrete terrace that is supposed to be private but isn't because it's right on the beach. My daughter likes to sit there looking at her computer all the time, to get away from me.'

Rose was in full flow as she made a list of her grievances. 'At night there are magic shows for the children on the beach. So much noise. The clattering of plates from the restaurants, the shouting tourists, the mopeds, the screaming children, the fireworks. I never get to the sea unless Sofia wheels me to the beach and it is always too hot anyway.'

'In which case I will have to bring the sea to you, Mrs Papastergiadis.'

Rose sucked in her bottom lip with her front teeth and kept it tucked like that for a while. Then she freed it. 'I find all the food here in southern Spain very hard to digest.'

'Sorry to hear that.' His blue gaze settled on her stomach like a butterfly landing on a flower.

My mother had lost weight in the last few years. She was shrinking and she seemed to have become shorter, because her dresses, once knee length, now fell just above her ankles. I had to remind myself that she was an attractive woman in early old age. Her hair, always styled in a chignon and held in place with a single hairpin, was her one expense. Every three months when the silver came through, it was wrapped in foils and lightened by a fashionable colour technician who had shaved off all her own hair. She had suggested I do the same to my wayward black curls which turned to frizz whenever it rained, which was often.

I regarded the hairdresser's shaving of her scalp as a ritual I could not participate in. At the time, I had wondered if she thought of her hair as the weight of the past and the shedding of it as a move towards the future, in the Hindu tradition, but she told me (a square of foil in her mouth) that she shaved her hair because it was less work. The weight of my own hair is the least of my burdens.

'Sofia Irina, sit down here.' Gómez patted the chair opposite his computer. He had casually called me by the full name written in my passport. When I sat down as instructed, he swung the screen round to show me a black-and-white image on the screen, with my mother's name written above it: R. B. PAPASTERGIADIS (F).

He was now standing behind me. I could smell a bitter herb in the soap he had used to wash his hands, perhaps sage. 'You are looking at a high-definition X-ray of your mother's spine. This is the back view.'

'Yes,' I said. 'I asked the doctors in Britain to send them to you. They are now out of date.'

'Of course. We will take our own and compare. We are looking for abnormalities, something out of the ordinary.' His finger moved from the screen to press the button on a small, grey radio standing on his desk. 'Excuse me,' he said. 'I want to hear what's happening with the austerity programme.'

We listened to a news broadcast in Spanish, interrupted now and again by Gómez, who told us the name of the Spanish financial analyst for the radio station. When Rose frowned, as if to ask what was going on – is he seriously a doctor? – Gómez dazzled us with his gold teeth.

'Yes, I am definitely a doctor, Mrs Papastergiadis. I wish to spend this afternoon going through your medication with you. I have the information of course, but I want you to tell me which of your medication you are most attached to and which you can let go. By the way, you will be pleased to know that the weather forecast says it will be dry and sunny in most parts of Spain.'

Rose shuffled in her wheelchair. 'I need a glass of water, please.'

'Very good.' He walked over to the basin, filled a plastic cup and carried it over to her.

'Is it safe to drink tap?'

'Oh yes.'

I watched my mother sip the cloudy water. Was it the right sort of water? Gómez asked her to stick out her tongue.

'My tongue? Why?'

'The tongue presents strong visual indicators of our general health.'

Rose obliged.

Gómez, who had his back to me, seemed to intuit that I was looking at the stuffed monkey on his shelf.

'That is a vervet from Tanzania. An electricity pylon killed him, then he was taken to the taxidermist by one of my patients. After some thought, I accepted his gift because vervet monkeys have many human characteristics, including hypertension and anxiety.' He was still staring intently at my mother's tongue. 'What we can't see is his blue scrotum and red penis. I think the taxidermist removed them. And what we have to imagine is how this boy played in the trees with his brothers and sisters.' He lightly tapped my mother's knee and her tongue slid back into her mouth. 'Thank you, Rose. You are right to ask for water. Your tongue tells me you are dehydrated.'

'Yes, I'm always thirsty. Sofia is lazy when it comes to putting a glass of water by my bed at night.'

'Where in Yorkshire do you come from, Mrs Papastergiadis?'

'Warter. It's a village five miles east of Pocklington.'

'Warter,' he repeated. His gold teeth were on full display. He turned to me. 'I think, Sofia Irina, that you would like to free our little castrated primate so he can scamper around the room and read my early editions of Cervantes. But first you must free yourself.' His eyes were so blue they could cut through a rock like a laser. 'I need to talk to Mrs Papastergiadis and make a treatment plan. It is something we must discuss alone.'

'No. She must stay.' Rose rapped her knuckles on one arm of her wheelchair. 'I will not be abandoning my medication in a foreign country. Sofia is the only person who knows all about it.'

Gómez shook his finger at me. 'Why would you want to wait in reception for two hours? No, what you must do is take the little bus which leaves from the entrance of my clinic. It will drop you near the beach in Carboneras. It is only a twenty-minute drive to town from the hospital.'

Rose looked affronted but Gómez ignored her. 'Sofia Irina, I suggest you make your way now. It is noon, so we will see you at two.'

'I wish I could enjoy a swim,' my mother said.

'It is always good to wish for more enjoyment, Mrs Papastergiadis.'

'If only.' Rose sighed.

'If only what?' Gómez knelt on the floor and placed his stethoscope on her heart.

'If only I were able to swim and lie in the sun.'

'Ah, how wonderful that would be.'

Again, I wasn't sure what to make of him. His tone was vague. Vaguely mocking and vaguely amiable. Which meant it was a bit bent. I reached for Rose's hand and pressed it. I wanted to say goodbye to her but Gómez was now listening with complete focus to her heart. I kissed the top of her head instead.

My mother said, 'Ouch!' She shut her eyes and leaned her head back as if she was in agony – or it might have been ecstasy. It was hard to tell.

*

The sun was fierce by the time I arrived at the deserted beach opposite the cement factory. I made my way towards a small café near a row of gas canisters and ordered a gin and tonic from the friendly waiter. He pointed to the sea and warned me not to swim because three people had been badly stung that morning by medusas. He had seen the welts on their limbs turn white and then purple. He grimaced and then shut his eyes and waved his hands as if to push away the ocean and all the medusas living in it. The gas canisters looked like strange desert plants growing out of the sand.

A large industrial cargo ship floated near the horizon. It was flying a Greek flag. I looked away and gazed instead at a rusty child's swing that had been hammered into the coarse sand. The seat was made from a battered car tyre and it was swaying gently, as if a ghostly child had recently jumped off it. Cranes from the desalination plant sliced into the sky. Tall undulating dunes of greenish-grey cement powder lay in a depot to the right of the beach, where unfinished hotels and apartments had been hacked into the mountains like a murder.

I glanced at my phone. There was an old text message from Dan who worked with me at the Coffee House. He wanted to know where I had put the marker pen we use to label the sandwiches and pastries. Dan from Denver was texting me in Spain about a pen? As I took a sip of my large gin and tonic and nodded my thanks to the waiter, I wondered if I had put the pen somewhere obscure.

I unzipped my dress so the sun could reach my shoulders. The burn of the medusa sting had calmed down, but every now and again I felt a twinge. It wasn't the worst kind of pain. In a way, it was a relief.

Another more recent message from Dan. He has found the pen. It turns out that while I am in Spain he is sleeping in my room above the Coffee House because his landlord put up his rent last week. The pen was in my bed. With the lid off. Consequently, the sheets and duvet are now stained with black ink. In fact, he described it as a haemorrhage of ink.

He can no longer write things like this:

Sofia's bittersweet Amaretto cheesecake – in £3.90, out £3.20.
Dan's moist orange and polenta cake (wheat- and gluten-free) –
in £3.70, out £3.

I am bittersweet.
He is moist.
Dan is definitely not moist.

We don't bake these cakes ourselves but our boss tells us that customers are more likely to buy them if they think we do. We put our names to things we do not make. I am glad the ink has run out of the lying pen.

I remember now that I must have left the pen in the bed when I used it to copy a quote from Margaret Mead, the cultural anthropologist. I wrote it straight onto the wall.

I used to say to my classes that the ways to get insight are: to study infants; to study animals; to study primitive people; to be psychoanalysed; to have a religious conversion and get over it; to have a psychotic episode and get over it.

There are five semicolons in that quote. I remember making the ;;;;; on the wall with the marker pen. I had underlined 'religious conversion' twice.

My father suffered a religious conversion but as far as I know he has not got over it. In fact he has married a woman four years older than I am and they have a new baby. She is twenty-nine. He is sixty-nine. A few years before he met his new wife, he inherited a fortune from his grandfather's shipping business in Athens. He must have seen it as a sign that he was on the right track. God brought him money just as his country was going bankrupt. And love. And a baby girl. I have not seen my father since I was fourteen. He has seen no reason to part with a single euro of his newly acquired wealth, so I am my mother's burden. She is my creditor and I pay her with my legs. They are always running around for her.

To sign off the loan to pay the Gómez Clinic we had to go together to Rose's mortgage provider for an interview.

I took the morning off work which meant I lost eighteen pounds and thirty pence for three hours. It was raining and the corporate red carpet was damp. Everywhere there were words on posters telling us how much our well-being meant to the bank, as if human rights were their major concern. The man sitting behind his computer had been trained to be cheerful and friendly; to imitate empathy as he understood it; to be approachable and energetic as he understood it; to love his ugly red tie with the bank's logo on it. His red badge displayed his name and job description, but it did not tell us his salary scale – probably somewhere in the region of dignified poverty. He was attempting to be personal; to be fair in his approach to our situation; to speak to us in simple language we would understand. A poster of three unattractive employees stared at us from the wall, all of them laughing. The woman was in a female suit (jacket with skirt), the men in male suits (jacket with trousers), their message conveyed our similarities and erased our differences; we are sensible dreamers with bad teeth just like you; we all want a place of our own to argue with the family on Christmas Day.

I could see that these posters were a rite of initiation (into property, investments, debt) and that the corporate suits signalled a sacrifice of the complexity of gender distinctions. Another poster displayed a photograph of a neat semi-detached house with a front garden the size of a grave. There were no flowers in that garden, just newly laid grass. It looked desolate. The squares of turf had not yet grown into each other. Perhaps a paranoid personality was lurking to the left of the story they were building for us. He had cut down all the flowers and murdered the household pets.

Our man spoke in a tone that was animated but robotic. At the start he said, 'Hi, you Guys,' but at least he did not say, 'Hello, Ladies,' before he rattled off the products available to strip me of my inheritance. At one point he asked my mother if she ate steak. It was a question out of the blue, but we could see where he was heading (lavish lifestyle) so Rose told him she was a vegan because she wanted to promote a more humane and caring world. If she was feeling extravagant, she said she'd add a tablespoon of yogurt to the dahl and rice. He did not know that vegans do not eat dairy products, otherwise she would have fallen out of the corporate red chair at the first hurdle. He asked if she liked designer clothes. She said she only liked cheap, ugly clothes. Did she belong to a gym? A strange question, given that my mother was clutching a walking stick and a bandage was wrapped around each of her swollen ankles, despite the anti-inflammatory painkillers she knocked back every morning with a glass of wrong water.

He asked her to provide the estate agents' estimate for our property and he informed us that the bank's own surveyor would pay us a visit. The computer liked the information we had submitted so far because my mother had paid off the mortgage. Bricks and mortar are worth something in London, even if the Victorian bricks are held together with spit, piss and gaffer tape. He told us he was inclined to sign off our loan. My mother was excited about having an adventure that included a medical experience: the Gómez Clinic was like whale watching for her. I returned to work to make three types of espresso and Rose returned home to make a new list of aches and pains. I can't deny that her symptoms are of cultural interest to me, even though they drag me down with her. Her symptoms do all the talking for her. They chatter all the time. Even I know that.

I walked across the burning sand to cool my feet in the sea.

Sometimes, I find myself limping. It's as if my body remembers the way I walk with my mother. Memory is not always reliable. It is not the whole truth. Even I know that.

When I arrived back at the clinic at 2.15, Rose had swapped the wheelchair for a chair and she was reading her horoscope in a newspaper for English expatriates.

'Hello, Sofia. I can see you have been having a nice time at the beach.'

I told her the beach was desolate and that I had been staring for two hours at a pile of gas canisters. It was my special skill to make my day smaller so as to make her day bigger.

'Look at my arms,' she said. 'I'm all bruised from the blood tests.'

'You poor thing.'

'I am a poor thing. The doctor has taken me off three of my pills. Three!'

She screwed up her mouth to make a mock-crying expression and then waved her newspaper at Gómez, who was not so much walking as promenading across the white marble floor towards us.

He told me that my mother has a chronic iron deficiency, which could be why she lacks energy. Among other things, such as a silver-lined dressing to enhance the healing of her foot ulcers, he had prescribed vitamin B12.

A prescription for vitamins. Is that worth twenty-five thousand euro?

Rose began to list the names of the pills that had been erased from her medication ritual. She spoke about them as if she were grieving for absent friends. Gómez lifted his hand to wave at Nurse Sunshine, who was making her way towards him in her grey suede heels. When she was standing by his side, he brazenly put his arm around her shoulders while she fiddled with the watch pinned above her right breast. An ambulance had just pulled up in the car park. She told him in English that the driver needed a lunch break. He nodded and removed his arm from her shoulders so she could get a better grip on the watch.

'Nurse Sunshine is my daughter,' he said. 'Her real name is Julieta Gómez. Please feel free to call her what you wish. Today is her birthday.'

Julieta Gómez smiled for the first time. Her teeth were blindingly white. 'I am now thirty-three. My childhood has officially ended. Please call me Julieta.'

Gómez gazed at his daughter with his eyes that were various shades of blue. 'You will know there is high unemployment in Spain,' he said, 'something like 29.6 per cent at the moment. So I am lucky my daughter had a good medical training in Barcelona and is the most respected physiotherapist in Spain. This means I am able to be a little bit corrupt and use my position to get her a job in my marble palace.'

He opened his pinstriped arms in a sweeping, royal gesture, as if to fold into himself the curved walls and flowering cacti, the shiny new ambulance, the receptionists and other nurses, and a couple of male doctors who unlike Gómez wore a uniform of blue T-shirts and brand-new trainers.

'This marble is extracted from the earth of Cobdar. Its colour resembles the pale skin of my deceased wife. Yes, I have built my clinic in homage to my daughter's mother. In the spring months we are enchanted by the abundance of butterflies that are attracted to my dome. They always lift the spirits of the afflicted. By the way, Rose, you might like to visit the statue of the Virgen del Rosario. She is sculpted from the purest marble from the Macael mountains.'

'I am an atheist, Mr Gómez,' Rose said sternly. 'And I do not believe that women who give birth are virgins.'

'But Rose, she is made from a delicate marble that is the colour of mother's milk. It is white, but slightly yellow. So perhaps the sculptor was merely paying his respects to the act of nurturing. I wonder, did the virgin's only child call his mother by her first name?'

'It doesn't matter,' Rose said. 'It's all lies, anyway. And by the way, Jesus called his mother "woman". It translates in Hebrew as "Madam".'

The receptionist suddenly appeared and started to speak very fast in Spanish to Gómez. She was carrying a fat white cat in her arms and she put it down on the floor by Gómez's polished black shoes. When it started to circle his legs he knelt down and stretched out his hand. 'Jodo is my true love,' he said. The cat rubbed its face against his open palm. 'She is very gentle. I am just sorry we do not have mice, because she has nothing to do all day long except to love me.'

Rose began to sneeze. After the fourth sneeze she clapped her hand to her eye. 'I am allergic to cats.'

Gómez slipped his little finger into Jodo's mouth. 'The gums should be firm and pink, and Jodo is okay in this respect. But her stomach is bulging in a new way. I am worried that she might have a kidney disease.'

He reached into his pocket, took out a bottle of sanitizer and sprayed it on his hands, while Julieta asked Rose if she would like some drops for her itching eye.

'Oh, yes, please.'

It's not often my mother says 'please'. She sounded as if she had just been offered a box of chocolates.

Julieta Gómez took out a small, white plastic bottle from her pocket. 'They are anti-histamines. I have just helped someone else with this problem.' She walked over to Rose, tipped her chin back and squeezed two drops into each eye.

My mother now looked daintily tearful, reproachful, as if the tears were welling but had not yet spilt on to her cheeks.

Jodo the cat had disappeared in the arms of one of the paramedics.

Nurse Sunshine, who was really Julieta, was neither friendly nor hostile. She was matter of fact, efficient, serene. She had none of her father's exuberance, although I observed that she listened very carefully to Rose, without appearing to do so. I was starting to rethink the way she had lingered by the door when we had walked into the consulting room. Perhaps she had not been as far away in her thoughts as I had imagined. She noticed things because she asked if she could help me do up my dress. I had forgotten I had loosened it at the beach.

Julieta fiddled discreetly with the zip, then placed her hands on her tiny waist and informed us that our taxi had arrived.

'Goodbye, Rose.' Gómez vigorously shook her hand. 'By the way, you should drive the hire car we have organized for you. It is included in my fee.'

'But how can I drive? I have no feeling in my legs.' Rose once again looked affronted.

'You have my permission to drive the car. Pick it up on your next visit. There is some paperwork to do, but it is ready for you in our car park.'

Julieta put her hand on my mother's shoulder. 'If you have any problems with the driving, Sofia can call us to come and fetch you. She has all our contact numbers.' The Gómez Clinic was obviously a family business.

Not only were we going to be provided with a car, Gómez informed my mother that he would be pleased to take her out for lunch. He asked Julieta to put a date in his diary for two days' time, bowed his silver head and turned on his heels to talk to one of the young doctors waiting for him by a marble pillar.

As I limped with Rose to the taxi, I asked her what kind of exercise Gómez had given her to do.

'It is not a physical exercise. He has asked me to write a letter in which I name all my enemies.' She snapped open her handbag and wrestled with a tissue that was stuck in the clasp. 'You know, Sofia, when Nurse Sunshine – or Julieta Gómez, or whoever she is – squeezed those drops into my eyes, I'm sure she smelt of alcohol. In fact, she smelt of vodka.'

'Well, it is her birthday,' I said.

The sea below the mountain was calm.

The Greek girl is lazy. The windows are dirty in their beach house but she has not cleaned them. She never locks the door. That is careless. It is like an invitation. It is like riding a bicycle without a helmet. That is careless too. It is an invitation to be hurt very badly should there be an accident.

Ladies and Gentlemen

The diving-school dog is already pulling at its chains and it's only 8 a.m. He stands on two legs and lifts his scabby brown head above the wall of the roof terrace, snarling at the beach life below it. Pablo is shouting at the two Mexican men painting the walls. They can't shout back because they don't have the right legal documents to give him the finger. The louder the dog howls, the louder Pablo shouts.

I am going to free Pablo's dog today.

I walk to Café Playa which is next to the diving school and order my favourite coffee, a cortado. Obviously, I want to inspect the way the waiter froths the milk, given that I was trained for six long days at the Coffee House to perfect my milk-foaming techniques. The waiter's black hair is gelled so that it sticks out in a number of directions. There are so many things his hair is doing with gravity. I could look at it for an hour instead of freeing Pablo's dog. The cortado is made with long-life milk, which is what they mostly use here in the desert. It is the sort of milk that is described as 'commercially stable'.

'We have travelled a long distance from the cow with a bucket of raw milk under its udder. We are a long way from home.'

This is what my boss told me, in her soft, sad voice, on my first day at the Coffee House. I still often think about it. I think about her thinking about it. Is home where the raw milk is?

The diving instructors are wheeling their plastic petrol canisters and oxygen tanks across the sand. Their boat is waiting for them in its specially roped-off part of the sea. When will it ever be the right time to free Pablo's dog?

I stand up to find the women's toilet and have to walk past the village alcoholic, who is eating a plate of luminous orange crisps with his morning cognac. The doors to the Señoras resemble the saloon swing doors of a bar in a cowboy movie, they are slatted and painted white. I've seen them in Westerns where the barkeeper stares suspiciously at the moody stranger when he makes his entrance. While I am peeing, someone walks into the next cubicle. There is a gap between the floor and the partition between the cubicles and I can see that this person is a man. He is wearing black leather shoes with gold buckles on the side. It's as if he's waiting for me. He is standing very still, I can hear him breathing, but he does not move his feet. He is lurking. I suddenly feel observed. Perhaps he can see me with my skirt hitched up round my waist. Why else is he just standing there? I wait a few seconds for him to make a move or to leave and when he doesn't I start to panic. I quickly pull down my skirt, push open the saloon door and run to find the waiter.

He is busy with the coffee machine and he's toasting bread and squeezing oranges at the same time.

'Sorry, but there's a man in the Señoras.'

The waiter grasps the cloth hanging over his shoulder and wipes the stainless-steel wand, which is dripping with milk. Then he turns round to take the stale baguettes off the grill and slides them on to a plate.

'What?'

My legs are shaking. I don't know why I am so frightened. 'There's a man in the Señoras. He was looking at me under the door. He might have a knife.'

The waiter shakes his head, irritated, he doesn't want to leave his machine with all the cups and glasses standing in a line under the steel tubes. It is complicated to make multiple coffees, each requiring a different shape of cup or a different kind of glass. 'Maybe you walked into the Caballeros? They are next to each other.'

'No. I think he's dangerous.'

He walks briskly with me to the door with 'Señoras' written underneath a roughly painted red lace fan and kicks it open.

A woman stands by the basin, washing her hands. She's about my age and she's wearing tight blue velvet shorts. Her blond hair is tied in a single thick plait. The waiter asks her in Spanish if she has seen a man in the Señoras. She shakes her head and continues washing her hands while the waiter nudges open the other door with his boot.

'The only man in here is you,' the woman says to the waiter. She's got a German accent.

I look down at the floor, humiliated, and while my eyes are down I see that the woman with the blond plait is wearing the men's shoes that I glimpsed in the other cubicle. Black leather shoes with gold buckles on the side. I don't know what to say, I'm blushing and I feel the same panic jitter again in my chest. The waiter flings up his hands and stamps out of the Señoras, leaving me and the woman alone.

We stand in silence and I wash my hands just to give myself something to do, but then I can't work out how to turn off the tap. She thumps it with her palm and the flow of water stops. When I look up at the mirror above the basins I can see her slanting green eyes looking at me. She is about my age. Her eyebrows are thick, almost black. Her hair is gold and straight.

'These are men's dancing shoes,' she says. 'I found them in the vintage shop up the hill. I work there.'

My wet fingers are now in my hair and I'm fidgeting with it. My curls start to frizz while she stands there calm and poised.

'I sew for the shop in the summer. They gave me these shoes.' She tugs at the end of her silky plait. 'I've seen you around with your mother.'

A man in the village square is shouting into a loudspeaker from his truck. He's selling melons and he's obviously in a bad mood because his hand is slammed on the horn.

'Yes. My mother is a patient at a clinic here.' I sound like such a loser. For some reason, I want her good opinion, but I'm not very impressive. My heart is still racing and there's water all over my T-shirt. She is tall and lean. Two silver bracelets circle her tanned wrists.

'I have a house here with my boyfriend,' she says. 'We come here most summers. I've got a pile of repairs to do for the shop today. After that we are driving to Rodalquilar for supper. I like driving at night, when it's cool.'

Her life is the sort of life I want. Her fingers are still stroking her plait.

'Are you going to drive your mother to see the sights?'

I explained how we have to pick up our hire car from the clinic but I don't drive and Rose has got problems with her legs.

'Why don't you drive?'

'I failed my test four times.'

'That's not possible.'

'And I failed my driving theory examination, too.'

She screwed up her lips and stared at my hair with her long-lidded, eyes. 'Can you ride a horse?'

'No.'

'I have been riding a horse since I was three.'

There was obviously nothing to recommend me to anyone.

'Sorry about the mix-up,' I said. I walked out of the Señoras as fast I could without actually running.

Where shall I go? I have nowhere to go. This is the fear the posters on the wall of my mother's mortgage company were signalling we shared. They are right. I walked to the plaza near the Café Playa to pretend to buy a watermelon.

I am saving the rinds for the chickens which are still, miraculously, laying eggs in the summer heat. They belong to Señora Bedello, whose husband died in the civil war, fighting Franco's fascist army.

It's not a man selling watermelons, it's a woman.

She's sitting in the driving seat of the van and she is beeping the horn with her small brown hand. I am so confused. I had an image in my mind of a sweaty male driver with stubble on his face, but she is a middle-aged woman in a straw hat. Her blue dress is dusty from the desert road and she's leaning her vast breasts against the steering wheel.

And then I remembered I hadn't finished my coffee.

I returned to Café Playa and gulped down my cortado like the village alcoholic downing his morning cognac.

There she is.

The woman in the men's shoes is standing by my table. Straight and tall, like a soldier girl. Looking out to sea. At the boats. At the children swimming in giant plastic rings. At the tourists who have laid out umbrellas and chairs and towels on the sand. The diving-school boat is now loaded with all its equipment and pulls away into the ocean. The brown Alsatian, who I have not yet freed, is still rattling his chains.

'My name is Ingrid Bauer.'

What is she doing standing so close to me?

'I am Sophie, but Sofia is my Greek name.'

'How do you do, Zoffie?'

The way she says my name is like a whole other life. I'm ashamed of my sad white flip-flops. They have turned grey in the summer.

'Your lips are splitting from the sun,' she says. 'Like the almonds split on the trees of Andalucía when they are ripening.'

Pablo's dog starts to howl.

Ingrid looks up at the diving-school roof terrace. 'That German shepherd is a working dog and should not be chained all day.'

'He belongs to Pablo. Everyone hates him.'

'I know.'

'I'm going to free the dog today.'

'Oh. How are you going to do that?'

'I don't know.'

She looks up at the sky. 'Will you make eye contact with him when you undo the chains?'

'Yes.'

'Wrong. Never do that. Will you make your body still like a tree when you approach him?'

'A tree is never still.'

'Like a log, then.'

'Yes, I will be still like a log.'

'Like a leaf.'

'A leaf is never still.'

She was still looking at the sky. 'There is a problem, Zoffie. Pablo's dog has been badly treated. He will not know what to do with his freedom. The dog will run through the village and eat all the babies. If you are going to unchain him, you will have to take him to the mountains and let him run wild. In that way he will be truly free.'

'But he will die in the mountains without water.'

Now she was looking at me. 'What is worse? To be chained all day with a bowl of water, or to be free and die of thirst?' Her left eyebrow was raised, as if to ask, *Are you a bit of a hysteric? You've had a waiter push open two doors to find a man who isn't there, you don't know how to turn off a tap, you don't know how to drive a car and you want to free a feral dog.*

She asked me if I wanted to walk on the beach.

I do.

I kicked off my flip-flops and we jumped over the three concrete steps that separate the café terrace from the beach. There was something about that jump, the fact that we did not walk down those steps, which made us both run at the same time. We ran fast across the sand, as if we were chasing something we knew was there but couldn't yet see. After a while we slowed down and walked along the shore. Ingrid took off her shoes and then she looked at me and threw them into the sea.

I heard myself shouting No No No. I hitched up my skirt and ran to grab them from the waves. When they were finally clasped to my chest, I walked out of the sea and gave them back to her.

She dangled one in each hand, shaking out the water and then she laughed. 'My God, these shoes. I didn't mean to frighten you, Zoffie.'

'It wasn't your fault. I was frightened anyway.'

Why did I say that? Was I frightened anyway?

We kept on walking, dodging the sandcastles that children were building with their parents, intricate kingdoms with turrets and moats. A girl of about seven was buried to her waist, her legs buried alive, while her three sisters sculpted a mermaid's tail. We jumped over her and started to run again until we arrived at the end of the beach. When I dropped on to a bank of black seaweed by the rocks, so did Ingrid Bauer. We lay on our backs, side by side, gazing up at a blue kite floating in the blue sky. I could hear her breathing. The kite suddenly crumpled and began its descent. I wanted my whole life so far to slip away with the rolling waves, to begin a different kind of life. But I didn't know what that meant or how to get to it.

A phone was ringing in the back pocket of Ingrid's shorts. She rolled on to her stomach to reach for it and I rolled over too, and then we moved closer. My cracked lips were on her full soft lips and we were kissing. The tide was coming in. I shut my eyes and felt the sea cover my ankles and what came to mind was the screen saver on my laptop, the constellations in the digital sky, the swirls of pink light which are gas and dust. The phone was still ringing but we kept on kissing and she was holding on to my shoulder with the medusa sting, squeezing the purple welts. It hurt but I didn't care, and then she broke away from me to answer her phone.

'I am on the beach, Matty. Can you hear the sea?' She held the phone towards the waves, but her slanting green eyes were looking at me. At the same time, her lips were mouthing, *I'm late, ve-ry late,* as if I was to blame for whatever it was that had made her late.

I was so confused I stood up and walked away.

When I heard her calling my name I did not turn round. The mermaid girl who had been buried in the sand by her sisters now had a full fan of a tail, decorated with shells and small pebbles.

'Zoffie Zoffie Zoffie.'

I kept on walking in a daze. I had made something happen. I was shaking and I knew that I had held myself in for too long, in my body, in my skin, the word anthropology from the Greek *anthropos* meaning 'human', and *logia*, meaning 'study'. If anthropology is the study of humankind from its beginning millions of years ago to this day, I am not very good at studying myself. I have researched aboriginal culture, Mayan hieroglyphics and the corporate culture of a Japanese car manufacturer, and I have written essays on the internal logic of various other societies, but I haven't a clue about my own logic. Suddenly that was the best thing that ever happened to me. What I felt most was the way she had squeezed the medusa sting on my shoulder.

She is drinking peach tea in the plaza and she is too hot because her blue and black checked shirt is for winter not for summer in Andalucía. I think she thinks she's a cowboy in her work shirt, always alone with no one to look at the mountain horizon at night and say my god those stars.

The Knocking

Tonight someone is tapping at the windows of our beach apartment. I have checked twice and no one is there. It might be the seagulls or the wind blowing sand from the beach. When I look in the mirror, I do not recognize myself.

I am tanned, my hair has grown longer and wilder, my teeth look whiter against my dark skin, my eyes seem bigger, brighter – all the better to cry with, because my mother is shouting at me, shouting things like, You haven't tied my shoelaces properly. Every time I run to kneel at her feet and tie them again, they come undone until I finally sit on the floor, put her feet on my lap and untie all the old knots to make new knots.

It was a long process of unpicking and unravelling and starting all over again. I asked her why she needed to wear shoes at all. Especially shoes with laces. It was night and she wasn't planning on going out.

'I can think better in shoes with laces,' she said.

She is reclining on a chair, staring at the whitewashed wall while I attend to her feet. If she let me turn the chair, she would be staring at the night stars. It would be the smallest movement to change her view but she is not interested. The stars seem to insult her. Every one of them offends her. She tells me she already has a view in her mind. It is of the Yorkshire Wolds. She is walking the trail, the grass is lush and springy, rain falls softly on her hair, it is the lightest rain and she has a cheese roll in her rucksack. I would like to do that walk with her in the Yorkshire Wolds, I'd be happy to butter the rolls and read the map. She half smiles when I tell her this but it's as if she has already forsworn her feet to someone else. I am nervous tonight. I can still hear someone tapping at the windows. It might be the mice that hide in the wall.

'You are always so far away, Sofia.'

It might be my father. He has come to look after my mother and give me a break. It might be a refugee who has swum to shore from North Africa. I will give her a home for the night. I would. I think I would do that.

'Is there water in the fridge, Sofia?'

I am thinking about the signs on the doors of toilets in public places that tell us who we are.

Gentlemen Ladies
Hommes Femmes
Herren Damen
Signori Signore
Caballeros Señoras

Are we all of us lurking in each other's sign?

'Get me water, Sofia.'

I am thinking about the way Ingrid held her phone out towards the waves. *I'm on the beach, Matty. Can you hear the sea?*

While she spoke to her boyfriend, she had placed her foot on the inside of my right thigh, just above my knee.

She had thrown her men's shoes on to the seaweed, where they swayed like small boats as the tide came in. The salty mineral smell of the dark, free-floating weed was enticing and intense.

I'm on the beach, Matty. Can you hear the sea?

The sea with all the medusas floating in it.

The sea that had soaked her blue velvet shorts.

I continue to unknot the old knots in my mother's laces and make new knots. There is definitely someone tapping at the windows. This time it's not so much a tap as a hard knock. I move my mother's feet from my lap and walk to the door.

'Are you expecting a visitor, Sofia?'

No. Yes. Maybe. Perhaps I am expecting a visitor.

Ingrid Bauer is wearing silver Roman sandals that lace up her shins and she is annoyed. 'Zoffie, I have been knocking for ever.'

'I didn't see you.'

'But I was here.'

She tells me that she has been talking over my situation with Matthew.

'What situation?'

'About having no transport. This is the desert, Zoffie! He has suggested he collect the car from the Gómez Clinic for you tomorrow.'

'It would be good to have a car.'

'Let me see your sting.'

I rolled up my sleeve and showed her the purple welts. They were beginning to blister.

She traced the sting with her finger. 'You smell like the ocean,' she whispered. 'Like a starfish.' Her finger was now in the crease of my armpit. 'Those little monsters really came after you.' She asked for my mobile number and I wrote it on the palm of her hand.

'Next time, Zoffie, open the door when I knock.'

I told her I never lock the door.

Our beach house is dark. The walls are thick to keep it cool in the summer heat. We often have the lights on in the day as well as at night. Not long after Ingrid left, all the lights suddenly went out. I had to stand on a chair and open the fuse box on the wall near the bathroom to flip the trip switch. The lights came back on and I climbed down to make Rose a pot of tea. She had packed five boxes of Yorkshire teabags and brought them with her to Spain. There is a shop at the end of our road in Hackney that stocks these teabags and she had walked to it to make her bulk purchase. Then she had walked back home. That is the mystery of my mother's lame legs. Sometimes they step out into the world like phantom working legs.

'Get me a spoon, Sofia.'

I got her a spoon.

I can't live like this. I must flip the trip in every way.

Time has shattered, it's cracking like my lips. When I note down ideas for field studies, I don't know whether I'm writing in the past or present tense or both of them at the same time.

And I still have not freed Pablo's dog.

When the Greek girl burns the coils of citronella at night to keep the mosquitos away I can see the curve of her belly and breasts. Her nipples are darker than her lips. She should give up the habit of sleeping naked if she does not want to be devoured by the mosquitos in the perfumed darkness of her room.

Bringing the Sea to Rose

I had promised to be totally silent at the table when Gómez took my mother to lunch. He had forbidden me to speak and asked for my trust in his judgement. In fact, he told me the staff would fetch Rose every day from the beach apartment and I was to do as I pleased. On Tuesdays he would call me into the clinic, given that I was my mother's next of kin. Apart from that, it was my choice. He wanted to get to know Rose, because her case truly puzzled him. It was not why she could not walk that interested him. He wanted to know why she could intermittently walk. This seemed like an affliction that might very well be physical, but one must not be a slave to medical theory. What did I think?

I regarded Gómez as my research assistant. I have been on the case all my life and he is just starting. There are no clear boundaries between victory and defeat when it comes to my mother's symptoms. As soon as he makes a diagnosis, she will grow another one to confound him. He seems to know this. Yesterday he told her to recite her latest ailment to the body of a dead insect, perhaps to a fly, because they are easy to swat. He suggested she surrender to this strange action and listen carefully to the monotony of the way it buzzes before it dies. It is likely, he said, that she will discover that the buzzing sound, often so irritating to the human ear, resembles the timbre and pitch of Russian folk music.

It is the first time I have ever seen her laugh out loud with her mouth open. At the same time, he has booked her in for various scans and his staff are attending to the silver-lined dressings on her right foot.

A table for three had been reserved in the village-square restaurant, because he assumed she could walk there with relative ease from the apartment. It had not been an easy walk. My mother had tripped over pistachio shells that had not been swept from the square the night before. I had spent an hour sorting out the laces of her shoes but, in the end, Rose had been felled by a nut that was no bigger than a large pea.

Gómez was already seated at the table. He sat opposite Rose and I sat next to him, as instructed. His formal pinstripe suit had been exchanged for elegant cream linen, not exactly informal but less businesslike than his first presentation of himself as a famous consultant. A yellow silk handkerchief was arranged in his jacket pocket in the old style, shaped into a round puff rather than folded at right angles. He was dapper, gentle and courteous. Both he and my mother peered at the menu and I just pointed to a salad, as if I were a mute out on a day trip. Rose took a while choosing a white-bean soup and Gómez flamboyantly ordered the house speciality, grilled octopus.

Rose rapidly informed him that she had allergies to fish and it made her lips swell. When he seemed not to understand, she leaned forward and poked my shoulder. 'Tell him about my fish problem.'

I said nothing, as instructed by Gómez.

She turned her attention to him. 'I cannot be in the vicinity of fish of any kind. The vapour from your octopus will waft towards me and I will come up in hives.'

Gómez nodded vaguely and reached for her hand. She was startled, but I think he might have been taking her pulse because I noticed he had a finger on her wrist. 'Mrs Papastergiadis, you take fish-oil supplements and you take glucosamine. I have had these analysed in our laboratory. Your brand of glucosamine is made from the outer coatings of shellfish. The other supplement you take is derived from shark cartilage.'

'Yes, but I am allergic to the other kind of fish.'

47

'A shark is not a shellfish.' His gold front teeth glinted in the sunshine. He had not reserved a table in the shade and the white stripe in his hair was damp from his sweat, which smelt of ginger.

When Rose reached for the wine list, he deftly grabbed it from her and moved it to the edge of the table. 'No, Mrs Papastergiadis. I cannot work with an intoxicated patient. If you were in my consulting room, I would not offer you wine. I have merely changed the venue. This is a consultation but I see no reason why it should not take place under the sky.'

He waved his hand and asked the waitress for a bottle of a particular mineral water which he told Rose was bottled in Milan then exported to Singapore and then exported to Spain.

'Ah, Singapore!' He clapped his hands, presumably to signal that he required more attention. 'I was very agitated at a conference in Singapore last month. I was advised to calm down by feeding the carp in the hotel fountain at breakfast and to look out at the South China Sea in the afternoon. Are those not beautiful words . . . "South China Sea"?'

Rose winced, as if the idea of anything beautiful was personally hurtful.

Gómez leaned back in his chair. 'In the rooftop pool of this hotel, the British tourists drank beer. They were up to their bellies in the water and they were drinking beer but they did not look out once on the South China Sea.'

'Drinking beer in a swimming pool sounds very nice to me,' Rose said sharply, as if to remind him that she was not a great fan of drinking water with lunch.

His gold teeth were like flames. 'You are sitting in the sunshine, Mrs Papastergiadis. The vitamin D is good for your bones. You must drink water. Now, I have a serious question. Tell me why you English say "wi-fi" and in Spain we say "wee-fee"?'

Rose sipped her water as if she had been asked to drink her own urine. 'Obviously, it's about a different emphasis on the vowel, Mr Gómez.'

A plastic boat was being inflated in the middle of the square by a thin boy of about twelve. His Mohican had been dyed green and he had his foot pressed against a plastic pump while he devoured an ice cream. Every now and again his five-year-old sister ran to the crumpled plastic to check the progress of its metamorphosis into something seaworthy. The waiter brought out the salad and bean soup, each plate balanced on the curve of his arm. He leaned over Gómez's shoulder to theatrically place a vast dish of purple-tentacled *pulpo alla griglia* on his paper mat.

'Oh yes, gracias,' Gómez said in his American Spanish accent. 'I cannot get enough of these creatures!' They place a vast dish of purple-tentacled *pulpo* on his paper mat. 'The marinade is its crowning glory . . . the chillis, the lemon juice, the paprika! I give thanks to this ancient inhabitant of the deep. Gracias, polpo, for your intelligence, mystery and remarkable defence mechanisms.'

Rose now had two red welts on her left cheek.

'Did you know, Mrs Papastergiadis, the octopus can change the colour of its skin to camouflage itself? As an American, I still find the polpo mysterious, a little *monstruo*, but the Spanish part of me finds it a very familiar monster.'

He picked up his knife and cut a blistered livid tentacle off the octopus. Instead of eating it, he threw it on to the ground, which was a blatant invitation to the cats in the village to join him for lunch. They started to circle his shoes under the table, coming from all directions to fight each other for a piece of the sea monster. He delicately sawed into the rubbery flesh of the polpo and pushed it into his mouth with relish. After a while he saw no reason not to drop three more tentacles into their paws.

My mother had become quiet and shockingly still. Not still like a tree or a leaf or a log. Still like a corpse.

'We were talking about Wi-Fi,' Gómez continued. 'I will tell you the answer to my riddle. I say "wee-fee" to rhyme with "Francis of Assisi".'

Three thin cats were now sitting on his shoes.

Rose must have been breathing after all, because she turned on him. The whites of her eyes were pink and swollen. 'Where did you go to medical school?'

'Johns Hopkins, Mrs Papastergiadis. In Baltimore.'

'Think he jests,' Rose whispered loudly.

I stabbed a tomato with my fork and did not respond. All the same, I was concerned about the way her left eye was closing up.

Gómez asked if she was enjoying her bean soup.

' "Enjoying" is too strong a word. It is wet but tasteless.'

'How is "enjoyment" too strong a word?'

'It is not an accurate word to describe my attitude to the soup.'

'I hope your appetite for enjoyment will get its strength back,' he said.

Rose rested her pink eyes on my eyes. I removed my gaze like a traitor.

'Mrs Papastergiadis,' said Gómez. 'You have some enemies to discuss with me?'

She leaned back in her chair and sighed.

What is a sigh? That would be another good subject for a field study. Is it just a long, deep, audible exhalation of breath? Rose's sigh was intense but not subdued. It was frustrated but not yet sad. A sigh resets the respiratory system so it was possible that my mother had been holding her breath, which suggests she was more nervous than she appeared to be. A sigh is an emotional response to being set a difficult task.

I knew she had been thinking about her enemies because she had written a list. Perhaps I am on that list?

To my surprise, her voice was calm and her tone almost friendly.

'My parents were my first adversaries, of course. They did not like foreigners so, naturally, I married a Greek man.'

When Gómez smiled his lips were black from the octopus ink.

He gestured to my mother to continue.

'Both my parents breathed their last holding the kindly dark-skinned hands of the nurses who tended them. But it seems churlish to have a go at them now. I will, anyway. To my parents on the Other Side. Remind me to spell for you the names of the hospital staff who sat with you on the day you died.'

Gómez rested his knife and fork on the edge of the plate. 'You are talking about your National Health Service. But I note that you have chosen some private care?'

'That is true and I feel a little ashamed. But Sofia researched your clinic and encouraged me to give it a go. We were at the end of the road. Weren't we, Fia?'

I gazed at the boat being pumped up in the square. It was blue with a yellow stripe across its side.

'So, you married your Greek man?'

'Yes, for eleven years we waited for a child. And when we at last conceived and our daughter was five, Christos was summoned by the voice of God to find a younger woman in Athens.'

'I am myself of the Catholic faith.'

Gómez shovelled more extraterrestrial octopus into his mouth.

'By the way, Mrs Papastergiadis, "Gómez" is pronounced "Gómeth".'

'I respect your beliefs, Mr Gómeth. When you get to heaven, may the pearly gates be draped in an octopus drying for your welcome dinner.'

He seemed up for everything she threw at him and had lost the chiding tone of their first meeting. Her eyes were no longer pink and the welts on her left cheek had subsided. ''Twas a long wait for my only.'

Gómez reached for the silk handkerchief arranged in a puff in his jacket pocket and passed it to her. 'God and walking. Maybe they are your enemies?'

Rose dabbed her eyes. 'It is not walking. It is walking out.'

I stared miserably at the cigarette butts on the floor. It was such a relief to be mute.

Gómez was gentle but persistent. 'This business with names. It's tricky.' He pronounced 'tricky' to rhyme with 'wee-fee'. 'In fact, I have two surnames. Gómez is my father's name, and my last name is my mother's name, Lucas. I have made a shorter name for myself but my formal name is Gómez Lucas. Your daughter calls you Rose but your formal name is Mama. It is uncomfortable, is it not, this to-ing and fro-ing between "Rose" and "Mrs Papastergiadis" and "Mother"?'

'It is very sentimental what you are saying,' Rose said, holding on tight to his handkerchief.

My phone pinged.

You now have car
Come get key
Parked near bins
Inge

I whispered to Gómez, telling him that the hire car had arrived and I needed to leave the table. He ignored me because his attention was entirely focused on Rose. I suddenly felt jealous, as if I were missing some sort of attention that had never been bestowed on me in the first place.

The car park was a square of dry scrubland at the back of the beach where the village dumped its garbage. The rancid bins were overflowing with decaying sardines, chicken bones and vegetable peel. As I walked through a black cloud of flies, I paused to listen to the buzzing.

'Zoffie! Quick, run. It's hot standing here.'

Their wings were intricate and oily.

'Zoffie!'

I started to run towards Ingrid Bauer.

And then I slowed down.

A fly had settled on my hand. I swatted it but I did not recite an ailment.

I made a wish.

To my surprise, the words I whispered were in Greek.

Ingrid was leaning against a red car. The doors were open and a man in his early thirties, presumably Matthew, was sitting in the driver's seat. At first he appeared to be staring intensely at himself in the mirror, but as I got closer I saw that he was shaving with an electric razor.

Something was sparkling on Ingrid's feet. She was wearing the silver Roman sandals that laced in a long criss-cross up her shins. She looked like she had been adorned with treasure. In ancient Rome, the higher the boot or sandal was laced up the leg, the higher the rank of the fighter.

In the dust and scrub of the car park I saw her as a gladiator fighting in the arena of the Colosseum. It would have been covered in sand to soak up the blood of her opponent.

'This is my boyfriend, Matthew,' she said. She gripped my sweaty hand in her cool hand and more or less pushed me into the car so that I fell on him and knocked the electric razor out of his hand. A sticker on the windscreen said 'Europcar'.

'Hey, Inge, go easy.'

Matthew's hair was blond like hers and fell to just below his jaw, which was still covered in shaving foam. I had fallen into his lap and we had to disentangle ourselves while his razor whirred on the floor of the Europcar. When I climbed back out to the putrefying stench from the bins, the sting on my arm was throbbing because I had knocked it against the steering wheel.

'Jeezus.' Matthew glared at Ingrid. 'What's going on with you today?' He picked up the razor and stepped out of the car. He switched it off and gave it to her to hold while he tucked his white T-shirt into the waistband of his beige chinos. He shook my hand. 'Hiya, Sophie.'

I thanked him for getting the car.

'Oh, it was no problem. A colleague I play golf with gave me a ride, which meant my lover girl could have a lie-in.' He draped his arm around Ingrid's shoulder. Even in flat sandals she was at least two heads taller than he was.

Half his jaw was still covered in foam. It looked like a tribal marking.

'Hey, Sophie, isn't the weather insane?'

Ingrid pushed his arm away and pointed to the Europcar. 'Do you like it, Zoffie? It's a Citroën Berlingo.'

'Yes, but I'm not sure about the colour.'

Ingrid knew I did not drive, so I wasn't sure why she had made such an effort to get the car on my behalf.

'Do you want to come over to our house and taste my lemonade?'

'I do, but I can't. I'm in the middle of lunch with my mother's doctor in the plaza.'

'All right. See you on the beach maybe?'

Matthew suddenly became energetic and amiable. 'I'll lock up the Berlingo when I've finished my insane electro foam shave and bring the keys and paperwork over to your table. By the way, why didn't they hire your mother an automatic? I mean, she can't walk, right?'

Ingrid looked annoyed but I couldn't work out why. When she playfully kicked his knee with the sole of her silver sandal, he grabbed her leg and then knelt down in the dust and kissed her tanned shins in the gaps between the criss-crossed straps.

When I got back to the plaza, my mother and Gómez seemed to be getting along. They were having an intense conversation and didn't take any notice when I returned to the table. I had to admit that Rose looked excited. She was flushed and flirtatious. She had even slipped off her shoes and was sitting barefoot in the sun. The shoes with the laces I had unknotted for an hour had been abandoned. It occurred to me that she had slept alone for decades. When I was five six seven I had sometimes crept into bed with her when my father left, but I remember feeling uneasy. As if she were folding her growing child back into her womb in the way an aeroplane folds its wheels back into its body after take-off. Now she was saying something about needing the three pills she has been asked to abandon and how coming to Spain to heal her lame legs was like crying for the moon. By which I think she meant we were searching for a cure that was beyond our reach.

If I were to look at my mother just once in a certain way, I would turn her to stone. Not her, literally. I would turn the language of allergies, dizziness, heart palpitations and waiting for side effects to stone. I would kill this language stone dead.

The thin boy with the Mohican was still inflating his boat. His brother was showing him the oars and they were having a heated discussion while their sister prodded the blue plastic dinghy with her bare foot. They were all excited about an adventure in the sea with a new boat. That was the right sort of thing to be excited by. It made a change from waiting for withdrawal symptoms.

Gómez's lips were black from the octopus he had eaten with such relish. 'So you see, Rose, I have brought the sea to you with my polpo, and you have survived.'

When Rose smiled, she looked pretty and lively. 'I have been robbed, Mr Gometh. I could have gone to Devon for less than one hundred pounds and sat by the sea with a packet of biscuits on my lap, patting one of many English dogs. You are more expensive than Devon. I am, frankly, disappointed.'

'Disappointment is unpleasant,' he agreed. 'You have my sympathy.'

Rose waved her hand to the waiter and ordered a large glass of Rioja.

Gómez glanced at me and I could see he was annoyed about the wine. The table was unsteady and had been wobbling all through lunch. He took a prescription pad out of his pocket, ripped off five of the scripts and folded them into a square. 'Sofia, kindly help me lift the table so I can wedge this under the leg.'

I stood up and gripped the edge nearest to me. It was surprisingly heavy for a table made from plastic. It was an effort to raise it half an inch off the ground while Gómez edged the paper into place.

Rose suddenly jumped. 'The cat scratched me!'

I looked under the newly steady table. A cat was sitting on her left foot.

Gómez tugged at the lobe of his left ear. I began to sense that he was taking mental notes, just as I had been doing all my life. If she had no feeling in her legs, her mind had made some claws that were pricking her feet.

It was like he was Sherlock and I was Watson – or the other way round, given I had more experience. I could see the sense of him testing her apparent numbness by inviting the village cats to join us for lunch. When I looked under the table again, I saw a tiny prick of blood on her ankle. She had definitely felt that claw dig into her skin.

Now I understood why he gave her permission to drive the hire car.

Someone was hovering by our table. Matthew, who was now clean-shaven, was standing behind my mother. 'Excuse me,' he said to Rose, as he leaned over her to pass me the car keys and a purple plastic wallet. 'You'll find all the paperwork in there.'

'Who are you?' Rose looked mystified.

'I am the partner of Ingrid, a friend of your daughter. She told me you were a bit strapped for wheels so I picked up the hire car for you this morning. It drives pretty smoothly.' He glanced at a cat chewing a polpo tentacle and grimaced. 'These street cats have diseases, you know.'

Rose blew out her cheeks and nodded slyly in agreement. 'How do you know this man, Sofia?'

I had been forbidden to speak so I was silent.

How did I know Matthew?

I'm on the beach, Matty. Can you hear the sea?

I'm on the beach, Matty. Can you hear the sea?

I need not have worried because Gómez took over.

He formally thanked Matthew for delivering the car to us and hoped that Nurse Sunshine had made sure the insurance was in order.

Matthew confirmed that all was well and that it had been a pleasure to walk through the 'insane' gardens of the clinic with the colleague who had been kind enough to give him a lift. He had more to say but was interrupted by my mother who was tapping his arm.

'Matthew, I need some help. Please escort me home. I need to rest.'

'Ah,' said Gómez. 'You could be lying in bed, resting! But why? It is not as if you have been breaking cobblestones with a pickaxe from dawn to dusk.'

Rose tapped Matthew's arm again. 'I can barely walk, you see, and I have just been attacked by a cat. Your arm would be appreciated.'

'Certainly.' Matthew grinned. 'But first I'm going to see off these scabby moggies.'

He stamped his brown two-tone brogues on the cement. With his pageboy haircut, he looked like a short European prince having a tantrum. All the cats ran off except one fearless tomcat, which Matthew started to chase in zigzags across the plaza. When he had seen it off he beckoned to my mother, who had already slipped on her shoes.

Matthew was standing four yards away from our table but he did not understand how long it would take Rose to walk to his arm. He glanced twice at the watch on his wrist while she hobbled in his direction. It was painful to witness the effort it took her to walk towards a man who did not particularly want her to arrive in the first place. At last she attached her arm to his arm.

'Have a good rest, Mrs Papastergiadis.' Gómez lifted his hand and waved two fingers in her direction.

When Rose turned round to take one last look at Gómez, she was appalled to see he was finishing off her soup.

After a while he congratulated me on my silence. 'You did not speak on your mother's behalf. That is an achievement.'

I was silent.

'You will notice how in anger, or perhaps with a sense of grievance, she is walking.'

'Yes, she does walk sometimes.'

'My staff will be conducting various investigations to test her bone health, in particular the spine, hips and forearms. But I observed that on the way to the restaurant, when she tripped, she did not strain or sprain or fracture anything at all. Osteoporosis can be ruled out on this observation alone. It is the vitality she puts into not walking that concerns me. I'm not sure I can help her.'

I was about to beg him not to give up on her but I hadn't got my voice back.

'Let me ask you, Sofia Irina, where is your father?'

'In Athens,' I croaked.

'Ah. Do you have a photograph of him?'

'No.'

'Why not?'

My voice had been seen off like the cat.

Gómez filled a glass with the water that was bottled in Milan but had something to do with Singapore and passed it to me. I took a sip and cleared my throat.

'My father has married his girlfriend. They have had a baby girl.'

'So you have a sister in Athens you have never met?'

I told him I have not seen my father for eleven years.

He seemed keen to reassure me that should I wish to visit my father, a rota of staff would be assigned to care for Rose every day.

'If you don't mind me saying, Sofia Irina, you are a little weak for a young healthy woman. Sometimes you limp, as if you have picked up on your mother's emotional weather. You could do with more physical strength. This is not a substantial table to lift, yet for you it was an effort. I do not believe you need to do more exercise. It is a matter of having purpose, less apathy. Why not steal a fish from the market to make you bolder? It need not be the biggest fish, but it must not be the smallest either.'

'Why do I need to be bolder?'

'That is for you to answer.' His tone was reassuring, calm and serious, considering he was probably mad. 'Now, there is something else I must talk to you about.' Gómez seemed genuinely upset. He told me that someone had graffitied a wall of his clinic with blue paint. It had happened this morning. The word painted on the wall was 'QUACK'. Meaning that he was a charlatan, a con man, not a reputable doctor. He thought it might have involved the friend of mine who came to collect the car. This man Matthew. Nurse Sunshine had given him the documents and keys and not long after he had left they had found the right side of the marble dome defaced with this word.

'Why would he do that?'

Gómez looked for the handkerchief in his jacket pocket and discovered it was not there. He wiped his lips on the back of his hand and then wiped his hand with a napkin. 'I am aware he plays golf with an executive for a pharmaceutical company which has been bothering me for some years. They have offered to fund research at my clinic. In return, they would be pleased if I were to buy their medication and prescribe it to my patients.'

Gómez was clearly distressed. He shut his agitated, bright eyes and rested his hands on his knees. 'My staff will clean the paint off the marble exterior, but I can only think that someone wants to discredit my practice.'

The Mohican boy and his little sister were now dragging the inflated blue boat across the square and down to the beach. Their brother followed them holding the oars.

Was Gómez a quack? Rose had already voiced this thought.

I no longer care about the twenty-five thousand euro we struggled to pay him. He can have my house. If he slaughters a deer and divines a walking cure from its entrails I would be grateful. My mother thinks her body is prey to malevolent forces, so I am not paying him to be complicit with her command on reality.

That evening when I was wandering around the village, I picked two sprigs of jasmine growing on a bush outside the house built halfway up the hill. A blue rowing boat was moored in the yard with the name 'Angelita' painted on its side. I crushed the fragile white petals in my fingers. The scent was like oblivion, a trance. The arch of desert jasmine was a coma zone. I shut my eyes and when I opened them again, Matthew and Ingrid were walking up the hill towards the vintage shop. Ingrid ran towards me and kissed my cheek.

'We're here to collect my sewing from the shop,' she said.

She was wearing an orange dress with feathers sewn around the neckline and matching peep-toe shoes.

Matthew caught up with her. 'Inge sewed her dress. I don't think she gets paid enough. I'm going to negotiate a raise for her.' He tucked his hair behind his ears and laughed when she punched him in the arm. 'You wouldn't want to be cursed by Inge. She's insane when she's angry. In Berlin she goes three times a week to her kick-boxing class, so don't mess with her.'

He walked over to the woman who owned the vintage shop, lit her cigarette and turned his back on us.

Ingrid reached out and touched my hair. 'You have a knot. I am embroidering two dresses with a stitch called a French knot. I have to wind the thread around the needle twice. When I've finished, I'm going to sew something for you.'

The feathers trembled against her neck as I pressed the jasmine under her nose.

A motorbike with two teenage boys perched on the seat roared past us.

'I think you picked those flowers for me, Zoffie.'

The smell of petrol and jasmine made me feel faint.

'Yes, I picked these flowers for you.'

I stood behind her and slid the petals into the band of her plait. Her neck was soft and warm.

When she turned round to face me, the pupils in her eyes were big and black as the sea glittering in the distance.

A Case History

Rose stands naked under the shower. Her breasts droop, her belly folds and folds again, her skin is pale and smooth, her silver-blond hair is wet, her eyes are bright, she loves the warm water falling on her body. Her body. What is her body supposed to want and who is it supposed to please and is it ugly or is it something else? She is waiting for withdrawal symptoms from the lack of the three pills that have been deleted from her list of medication. So far they have not arrived. Yet she continues to wait for them like a lover, nervous and excited. Will she be disappointed if they don't turn up?

Today, Julieta Gómez is going to take a case history of Rose's body and I have been asked to be present. Where does a case history start?

'It starts with family,' Julieta Gómez says. 'It is a history.' She has swapped her dove-grey heels for trainers. Her thin chiffon blouse is tucked into tailored trousers which press tight against her hips. She walks Rose to a chair in the physiotherapy room and sits opposite her. 'Are you ready to make a start?'

Rose nods while Julieta fiddles with a small sleek black box lying between them on the desk. She had reassured my mother that this device was used for all the clinic audio archiving and that it was confidential. So now the volume levels were set. Apparently they would both soon forget that their conversation was being recorded.

Julieta spoke first to give some facts. She noted the date, the time, my mother's name, age, weight and height.

I sit uneasily in the corner of the physiotherapy room with my laptop on my knees, floating out of time in the most peculiar way. It seems wrong, even unethical, to have asked me to be there but I had agreed to Gómez's request on the understanding that apart from Tuesdays I would be free for the rest of the treatment. I have to pay for my freedom by listening to my mother's words.

She is speaking.

Her father had a temper problem. Which can be confused with having high levels of energy. Which can be confused with being manic. He needed no more than two hours of sleep a night. Her mother suffered from her father. Which can be confused with depression. She needed no less than twenty-three hours of sleep. I know this history but I don't want to be connected to it. I put on my headphones and gaze at YouTube on my shattered screen with all my life in it. Some of that life is the thesis for my abandoned doctorate that is lurking under the digital constellations made in a factory on the outskirts of Shanghai.

Now and again I lift off the headphones.

My mother is giving a history of her present illness. Where does that history start? It moves around in time and merges into past history, childhood illness and all the rest of it. This is not chronological time. Julieta will have to later transcribe Rose's words and author her case history. I have been trained to do something similar, except I am not a physiotherapist, I am an ethnographer. Julieta will at some stage have to describe the complaint that brought the patient to her clinic. Symptoms and their presentation. It is not one complaint. It is not even six. I overheard twenty complaints but there were more. The past the present and the future are simultaneously present in all these complaints.

Rose's lips are moving and Julieta is listening but I'm not listening. I have been asked to be present but I am not present. I'm watching a Bowie concert from 1972 on YouTube and it is buffering while he sings. His hair is red like a blood orange, his glitter shirt is

sparkling darkly to trigger associations of space travel and his platform shoes are stacked high to lift him off Earth. Bowie's painted
eyelids are silver spaceships. Girls are screaming and crying and
stretching out their hands to touch the Space Oddity strutting the
stage. He is a freak, like the medusa. The girls are feral and fertile
and freaked out.

We are so pinned down on Earth.

If I had been there, I would have been the loudest screamer.

I am still the loudest screamer.

I want to get away from the kinship structures that are supposed
to hold me together. To mess up the story I have been told about
myself. To hold the story upside down by its tail.

Rose is coughing. A pattern is emerging where she always coughs
when she is about to reveal something awkward and intimate. As if
the cough is a plunger unblocking memory. She is giving a case history. Sometimes I can hear a few sentences. I am becoming interested
in Julieta Gómez's interviewing style. Anthropologists might describe
it as 'in-depth interviewing'. My mother would be called 'the informant'. I notice her questions are minimal but my mother's emotions are
running high. I wish I was somewhere else. Julieta is relaxed but alert,
she never seems to pry or push and she is not in a rush to fill in the
silences. I have heard tapes where ethnographers have probed too
deeply into the informants' stories and made them silent, but my
mother's lips are mostly moving. 'Physiotherapy' does not seem
an accurate description of the kind of conversation that is taking
place. Perhaps Rose's memories are in her bones. Is that why bones
have been used as divination tools from the beginning of human
history?

My mother has a lot of contempt for her body. 'They should just
cut off my toes,' she says.

Julieta has finished the first case history and is helping her to stand
up. 'Move your left foot.'

'I can't. I can't move my left foot.'

'You need to do some weight-bearing exercise for strengthening and endurance.'

'My whole life has been about endurance, Nurse Sunshine. Remember that my first enemy and adversary is endurance.'

'How do you spell that in English?'

Rose tells her.

Julieta's hands are now under Rose's chin as she helps align her head.

Rose is looking for her wheelchair, which seems to have disappeared from the room.

'Everything hurts. I might as well do away with these useless feet. It would be a relief.'

Julieta looked at me. Her eyelashes were mascaraed into spikes. 'I think Rose does not stand up straight because she is tall.'

'No, I hate these feet,' my mother shouted at her.

Julieta led her back to the wheelchair which had now materialized, carried in by a porter who was trying to read the newspaper he had balanced on the armrest. On the front page was a photograph of Alexis Tsipras, the Prime Minister of Greece. I noticed he had a cold sore on his bottom lip.

'Cut off my feet, that's what I want,' my mother told Julieta.

In reply, Julieta gave the wheelchair a deft kick with her left trainer. 'What is your point, Rose?'

My mother started to make small circles with her shoulders, moving them forwards then backwards as if limbering up for a wrestling match. 'There is no point.'

Julieta looked pale and exhausted. She walked over to me and gave me what looked like a business card. 'Come and see me in my studio, if you like. I live in Carboneras.'

I was still puzzling over this when Gómez entered the room, followed by his white cat, Jodo. The stripe in his hair matched Jodo's white fur. The cat was plump and serene, purring loudly at her master's feet.

'How is your physiotherapy, Mrs Papastergiadis?'

'Call me Rose.'

'Ah yes, it is good to let these formalities go.'

'If you forget things, Mr Gómez, write them down on the back of your hand.'

'I will,' he said.

Julieta told her father she had taken the first case history and now she was tired and would like twenty minutes to have a coffee and a pastry. Gómez lifted his hand and smoothed down his vivid white streak. 'There is no such thing as tired so early in the day, Nurse Sunshine. The young do not rest. The young must be up all night with the lighthouse keepers. The young must argue till dawn.'

He asked her to repeat to him the relevant sections of the Hippocratic oath. She walked to the recording device and turned it off. 'I will prescribe regimens for the good of my patients according to my ability and my judgement and never do any harm to anyone,' she said gloomily.

'Very good. If the young are tired, they must improve their lifestyle.'

It seemed as if he was chastising her in some way. Had he somehow seen the kick his daughter had lashed out at the wheelchair?

Gómez's attention was entirely focused on my mother. He was taking her pulse but from a distance it looked quite intimate, as if they were holding hands. His voice was gentle, even flirtatious. 'I note you are not using the car yet, Rose.'

'No. I will need to practise before I drive Sofia on these mountain roads.'

His fingers pressed lightly on her wrist. They were still, but moving. Like a leaf. Like a stone in a stream.

'You see, Sofia Irina, Mrs Papastergiadis is concerned for your safety.'

'My daughter is wasting her life,' Rose replied. 'Sofia is plump and idle and she is living off her mother at quite an advanced age.'

It is true that I have shape-shifted from thin to various other sizes all my life. My mother's words are my mirror. My laptop is my veil of shame. I hide in it all the time.

I tucked it under my arm and walked out of the physiotherapy room. Jodo followed me for a while. Her paws were soft and soundless, and then she disappeared. I must have taken a wrong turning because I was lost in a labyrinth of milky marble corridors. I began to feel smothered by the veined walls, as if they were closing in on me. The echo of my heels hitting the marble floor reminded me of that first visit to the clinic, when I heard the amplified echo of Julieta's heels as she ran away from her father. Now I was running away from my mother. It was a relief to find the glass exit, to at last breathe in the mountain air and stand among the succulents and mimosa trees.

In the distance below the mountain I could see the ocean and a yellow flag planted in the coarse sand on the beach. It was like a haunting, that flag. Where would the Medusa's case history begin and end? Was she shocked, devastated, appalled to discover she was no longer admired for her beauty? Did she feel de-feminized? Would she walk through the door labelled 'Ladies' or the door labelled 'Gentlemen'? 'Hommes' or 'Femmes', 'Caballeros' or 'Señoras'? I began to wonder if she had more power in her life as a monster. Where had I got to in my own life by trying to please everyone all the time? Right here. Wringing my hands.

A blast of fine sand lashed my cheeks. It was as if the sky had opened and it was raining sand. I saw a flash of white fur as Jodo ran for cover under the silver leaves of a succulent that was shaped like an umbrella. A male cleaner in overalls and a protective eye shield was hosing down the wall near the exit to the clinic. After a while I realized that it was not water pouring through his hose. He was sandblasting the wall. As I walked closer I saw that three words had been spray-painted in blue on the walls. They were fading now, so the cleaner had obviously tried more than once to remove them. Was this the graffiti that Gómez had referred to a few days earlier? But it did not say 'QUACK'. I could clearly see the shape of the letters, despite the effort that had gone into erasing the paint. Gómez had obviously wanted to demonstrate that he knew my mother thought he was a quack. As if the thought had already committed the crime and defaced the walls of his clinic. The blue grafitti was not one single word. It was three words.

SUNSHINE IS SEXY

She wears a sombrero some days, drifting around. No one to row her in a boat to the smaller bays, no one to hear her say the water's so clear here oh wow I'm going to dive for that sea star. It has come to my attention that she has two credit cards to help her get through the month. Maybe I should offer to lend her some money?

Hunting and Gathering

'Why do you want to kill a lizard?'

Ingrid was crouching in an alleyway near the pizzeria that is owned by a Romanian taxi driver. At first I couldn't work out what she was doing and then I saw she was holding a miniature bow and arrow. It was so tiny it could fit in the palm of her hand. She was aiming the arrow at a lizard that had just flashed out of a crack in the wall. The arrow hit the wall and fell to the ground.

'Zoffie! Your shadow distracted me. My aim is usually right on target.' She picked up the arrow, which was sharpened to a point the size of a pencil, and showed me the little curved bow with its taut nylon string.

'I made it myself from bamboo.'

'But why do you want to kill a lizard?'

She prodded the white cardboard box I had left near the wall.

'It seems like I'm always freaking you out, Zoffie. What's in your box?'

'A pizza.'

'What kind of pizza?'

'Margarita with extra cheese.'

'You should eat more salad.'

Ingrid's long hair is pinned up on top of her head. She looks like a statue, strong and toned in her white cotton dress with its criss-crossed straps. Her plimsolls are white, too. When the lizard scuttled out of the crack again, she gestured for me to get out of the way. It had a green tail and blue circles on its back.

'Move! Go away, Zoffie, I'm working. Have you freed Pablo's dog yet?'

'No. He sacked one of the Mexican painters this morning. Pablo still owes him money.'

'He'll never get paid, Zoffie. Get a thicker skin, like our friend the lizard.'

I asked if I could take a photo of her with the bow and arrow.

'Go ahead.'

I took out my iPhone and aimed it at her head.

Who is Ingrid Bauer?

What are her beliefs and sacred ceremonies? Does she have economic autonomy? What are her rituals with menstrual blood? How does she react to the winter season? What is her attitude to beggars? Does she believe she has a soul? If she does, is it embodied by anything else? A bird or a tiger? Does she have an app for Uber on her smartphone? Her lips are so soft.

I pressed the time-lapse icon, then Slo-mo and then just Photo. Through the lens I could see her opening the box and taking out the pizza. She frowned at the congealed orange cheese and threw it to the ground.

'I would rather eat the lizard. Have you finished taking the photo?'

'Yes.'

'What are you going to do with it?'

'I will remember August in Almería with you.'

'Memory is a bomb.'

'Is it?'

'Yes.'

'What are you going to do with the lizard when you catch it?'

'Study the geometry of its patterns – they give me ideas for my embroidery. It will come out of the wall soon. Move! Move!'

When I did not move she ran towards me in her white plimsolls as if she was going to attack me. Her arms were around my waist as she lifted me high above her head and then she let me drop down and her hand looped up the hem of my dress. I felt her shaking as blossoms drifted down from the jacaranda tree behind the wall.

'You are a monster, Zoffie!' She pulled away from me and kicked the pizza box out of her way. 'Go and study a Stone Age settlement, or something. Don't you have work to do?'

I do have work to do. I am studying Ingrid Bauer's bow and arrow. It is magnifying in my mind until it becomes a weapon that can wound its prey. The bow is shaped like lips. The arrow's tip is sharp. Why am I a monster to Ingrid? She thinks of me as some sort of creature. I am her creature. The tip of the arrow is aimed at my heart.

I felt very light. Like an arrow in flight.

It was late afternoon and the beach was empty. I waded into the warm oily sea, for once not crowded with lilos and plastic boats. I told myself I was going to swim to North Africa which I could see across the horizon in vague outline. Heading for a whole other country was my way of doing the crawl for a long stretch, aiming for somewhere impossible to get to. The water became clearer and cleaner the further I swam out. After about thirty minutes I turned on my back and floated under the sun, my lips cracking all over again from the salt and heat.

I am far away from shore but not lost enough. I must return home but I have nowhere to go that is my own, no work, no money, no lover to welcome me back. When I flipped over I saw them in the water, the medusas, slow and calm like spaceships, delicate and dangerous. I felt a lashing, burning pain just under my left shoulder and started to swim back to shore. It was like being skinned alive as I was stung over and over again. When I limped across the sand towards the injury hut on the beach, the bearded student seemed to be expecting me because he was waiting with his tube of special ointment in his hand. I turned around to show him my shoulder and heard him say, 'That is bad, very baaaad.' He stood behind me and his fingers were on the stings. It was agony but he was touching me very lightly, moving the ointment in circles, and he spoke in a voice that started off soothing, like a mother, perhaps, I don't know.

'I saw you swim out. Did you not see the flag?' His voice became higher. 'I was calling to you, Sofia.'

He remembered my name.

'Sofia Papastergiadis. Are you breathing?'

'No.'

'You are crazy to swim so far out when the flag is up.'

He was shouting, like a brother, perhaps like a lover, I don't know. Something weird was happening because I wanted to pull him down to the floor and make love to him. I had been stung into desire. An abundance of desire. I was turning into someone I did not recognize. I was terrifying myself.

He took my hand and helped me on to a low table. I lay on my right hip – there was no way I could lie on my back – and he gave me a thin cushion for my head. When he drew up a chair and sat at my side I was so turned on by the way he was stroking his beard. The sting was electrifying me. I heard a swoosh. He was standing now, washing the sand off my feet with a bucket of water. I wanted him to climb on to the table and cover my body with his and I wanted to wrap my legs around his waist like a lover and I wanted to give him so much pleasure he would scream the injury hut down. Instead, he gave me the form to fill in.

Name:
Age:
Country of origin:
Occupation:

This time I left everything blank, except under Occupation I wrote Monster. He looked at the form and then at me. 'But you are a beautiful woman,' he said.

The night was humid and windless. I couldn't sleep. There was no position that did not chafe the tender stings on my shoulders and back and thighs. I had thrown my sheet on to the floor. Weak and thirsty, I must have been hallucinating because I saw my mother standing by my bed. She seemed very tall. The bed sheet was lifted from the floor and folded gently over my body. A male voice close to my ear began to whisper in Spanish, telling me to visit the salt-mining town of Almadraba de Moltelva, the palms in Las Presillas Bajas and the black mountains in El Cerro Negro. It might have been the student from the injury hut. Two hours later, in my delirium, I could smell Matthew's cologne. He had been on my mind ever since I saw the graffiti on the clinic wall. Someone else was in my room, breathing, lurking. I fell asleep and when I woke up I saw a woman with blond hair curled up at the ends like an old-fashioned movie star. She wore a backless red evening dress and she was holding a jar in her gloved hands.

'Zoffie, let me see your new stings.'

I lifted up my shirt.

'Oh, you poor girl, those sea monsters are evil. You're really in the wars.'

Rose was calling from the next room. 'Sofia, someone is in the house.'

I pulled the sheet over my head.

Ingrid pulled the sheet off my head. 'Have you told your mother you never lock the door?'

'No.'

Ingrid took off the white glove on her right hand. 'I've brought you manuka honey for your cracked lips.' She dipped her finger into the jar and smeared it on my lips. 'You are getting too brown, Zoffie.'

'I like being brown.'

'Where is your father?'

'Athens. I have a new sister. She's three months old.'

'You have a sister? What is her name?'

'I don't know.'

'I have a sister, too. She lives in Düsseldorf.' She took a deep breath and blew across my stings. 'Does that feel nice?'

'Yes.'

She told me she was on her way to a 1930s party at the vintage shop. An orchestra from Almería was going to play all the old tunes. She hoped I would hear the music from my sickbed and think of her and she would pick some desert jasmine and think of me. She stroked my shoulder with the white glove. 'Do you like the taste of the honey?'

'Yes.'

She told me how she knew the steps to all the 30s dances but she would prefer to gallop on a horse in the mountains because she had too much energy for slow dancing. 'Shall I lie with you for a while, Zoffie?'

'Yes.'

'You are a monster,' she whispered.

She leaned over me and licked the honey off my lips. When she stood up, the pleats of her red dress touched the tiles on the floor. She remained very still for a long time.

After a while I began to feel the same sort of panic I had experienced in the Señoras the day I first met her. I wanted her to leave but I didn't know how to ask her to go. When I told her I would have to get my mother some water, she laughed in the dark. 'If you want me to go away, why don't you say so?'

Two flies circled my lips. I need to be bolder. I don't want her to lurk in the dark. It is so hard to say out loud the things I want to say.

'Will you visit me in Berlin?'

'Yes.'

She was whispering again as she stood over me like a glamorous mourner at a wake. She wanted me to spend Christmas with her and she would pay for my flight. Berlin was cold in winter. I was to bring a heavy coat and she would take me for a ride in one of those horse-drawn carriages. They were for tourists but she liked them, especially when it was snowing. The ride would start at the Brandenburg Gate and move on to Checkpoint Charlie. She would hold a sprig of mistletoe above my head and I would obey the ritual. It was as if she was implying that the mistletoe would lead me to her lips, and not my own free will.

'Will you ride in a stupid carriage with me?'

'Yes.'

'Is okay with you that I visited so late?'

'Yes.'

'Are you happy we have met, Zoffie?'

'Yes.'

She walked out of my room and let herself out through the unlocked door.

Boldness

The local fish market turned out to be near the Romanian pizzeria in the basement of a block of apartments. Not many tourists knew it was there, but when I walked in there was already a crowd of women from the village buying the day's catch.

Gómez had suggested I steal a fish to achieve more courage and purpose. I regarded this task as an anthropological experiment, though it crossed a border into something approaching magic, or perhaps magical thinking. When I googled how to gut a fish, there were over 9 million results.

The first fish to snare my attention from the point of view of a thief was a monkfish with a monster face, mouth gaping open to reveal its two rows of sharp little teeth. I lightly poked my finger into its mouth and discovered a world that was totally unknown to me, like Columbus discovering the Bahamas. The cashier, a fierce woman in a yellow rubber apron, shouted in Spanish not to touch the fish. Already I had made myself visible, when the point of a thief is to slip unseen into the night and not into the mouth of a fish. I had slung a basket bag with leather straps over my shoulder and it chafed the stings, which were now raised welts, a sprawling, crazy web of tattoos inked in venom. The cashier, who was now weighing three mackerel on an old-fashioned brass scale, had her eye on everyone, including the criminal in the room. This catch was her livelihood, she would pay her sea hunters from the sale of their hard-won bounty, but I couldn't think about that now.

I walked towards the silver sardines. I could easily steal one but that would be a token, not worth the risk. Women were frowning and shaking their heads at the scales, as if they couldn't believe what it told them. Sometimes they included me in this conversation, throwing up their hands in mock-despair at the heaviness of fish which looked deceptively delicate.

I considered the whiskery langoustines, pale grey with protruding, black, beady eyes. They were the professors of the ocean but they did not make me feel bolder. A huge tuna lay on a bed of ice. What if I slipped it into my basket? It wouldn't fit. I would have to pick it up with both hands, clasp it to my chest and run with my eyes shut into the village and see what happened next. It was the most precious jewel in the market, the emerald of the sea. My hand reached towards it, but I couldn't follow it through. A tuna was too ambitious, not so much bold as reckless.

Ingmar's Swedish girlfriend, who owned one of the more expensive restaurants on the beach, walked in and shouted her greetings to the crowd. Someone complimented her on her turquoise suede shoes, which had a row of gold bells sewn across the toes. She was young and wealthy so everyone knew she was going to barter a good deal for her restaurant. She wore a pink crocheted dress and her lips were lined with pink pencil so they were just an outline. I don't know why someone would want an outline for lips. She commanded the cashier to scoop up the three lobsters and the monkfish and heave the tuna on to the scales. Her voice was too loud. Perhaps she couldn't hear herself, but we could hear her. The bells on her shoes jangled every time she changed the position of her feet. She was making her offer for the tuna, everyone was listening, and then she delivered her threat. As she barely made a profit, it stood to reason that if the price wasn't friendly she would buy all her fish in Almería.

Obviously, raising the voice compels attention and incites fear, but was she bold? Did I want to be bold like her? What shade of bold was I after?

I moved away from her elbows to get a better look at the pile of slimy octopus, the polpo that Gómez had eaten with such relish. It would be relaxing to steal because it was shapeless and soft. I slipped my basket under the marble slab and mentally prepared myself to slide the polpo in with my hand. I paused. It did not make me feel bold so much as uneasy. If it was alive, it would change its identity and imitate its predator. It might even mimic the colour and texture of my human skin, which can also change colour, in excitement, in humiliation or fear. Its skin could express mood, it could blush like I always blush when I am asked to spell my name. I felt ashamed to look into its clever, dead, strange eyes with the pupils dilated, so I looked away and that's when I saw my fish. It was looking straight at me and its eyes were furious. It was a plump dorado in a rage. I knew it was destined to be mine.

Ingmar's girlfriend was helpful to me because everyone's attention was on her. She did not inspire affection in her community. She was audacious but she was not bold.

To steal the dorado, I had to conquer my fear of being found out and shamed. I relaxed all my muscles until I was as still as a leaf – perhaps as still as a tea leaf, which is cockney rhyming slang for 'thief'. Very slowly, I moved closer to the dorado, and with my left hand I touched the price tag on the langoustines to distract the cashier from my right hand, which was sliding the grumpy dorado into my basket.

As far as I could make out, this was the model that most politicians had adopted to run their democracies and dictatorships. If the reality of the right hand is being messed up with the left hand, it would be true to say that reality is not a stable commodity. Someone banged my back, quite close to my stings, but I took no notice and walked straight out of the door. I noted that I did not loiter and that I had a new sense of purpose and intention. My sense of purpose was quite loud. It had closed all the portals to my senses, nostrils, eyes, mouth, ears. I had become single-minded, blinkered to everything else going on. A sense of purpose requires the subject to lose some things and gain others, but I wasn't sure it was worth it.

Standing in the kitchen in the beach apartment, I grasped the dorado by the tail and stared back at it. Yes, it was still furious. Its mood had not changed. It was heavy. Plump and shiny and sleek. It was a big fish. I took off my shoes and let my toes spread on the floor. The diving-school dog howled miserably while I felt all of gravity pulling me down. I held the fish by its head and scraped at the scales with a blunt knife. Pablo's dog was going berserk, he did not leave a second of silence between one bark and the next. I placed the fish on its side, inserted the knife into its tail and slid it all the way to the head. The Greek side of my family, from Thessaloniki, did not need Google to tell them how to gut a fish. I opened its belly and cut away at the guts, which were white and slimy. The ancient Greek side of my family would have caught plaice in the shallows of the Aegean. The Yorkshire side of my family bought fish from the trawlermen at the docks, men who had survived the arctic seas and were on deck for ten hours in the raw winds.

There was a lot of blood in this fish. My hands were dripping with it. If someone had banged on the door to claim their stolen goods, I would literally have been caught red-handed.

The miserable Alsatian had found new howling energy. He was unstable and he was tipping me into complete lunacy. I threw down the knife and ran barefoot across the sand to the entrance of the diving school, pushing open the door with my blistered shoulder.

PABLO PABLO PABLO. Where is he?

Pablo was bent over his computer with a glass of vermouth in his hand. A heavy, middle-aged man with thick, greasy black hair parted at the side, he looked up at me with his big, sleepy brown eyes, and he flinched.

'Untie your dog, Pablo.'

A mirror was hanging on the wall behind him. My cheeks were

marked with streaks of fish blood and some of the entrails were caught in my hair, which had become a coarse tangle of knotted curls from swimming every day. I looked like some sort of sea monster rising from the shells and starfish that decorated the mirror's frame. I was terrifying myself all over again and I was terrifying Pablo.

He moved his chair, as if preparing to run, and then he must have changed his mind because he sat down again and lifted his hand up to his eyes. He wore a gold ring on his little finger. His flesh seemed to be growing over the band of gold.

'If you do not leave my property,' he said, 'I will call the police.'

I strained to hear the rest because the dog had accelerated his bid for freedom, but it was something like 'The cop in this village is my brother and the cop in the next village is my cousin and the cop in Carboneras is my best friend.'

I grabbed his hand, with the gold embedded in it, and pressed my forehead to his forehead while his right hand groped for something under his desk. Perhaps it was a panic button wired to his extended family of cops. He asked me to get out of his way so he could walk up the stairs to the roof terrace.

I took a step backwards. He was a big man. To steady myself, I pressed my hand against the newly painted white wall while I waited for him to move. It left a bloody handprint, and so I made another. And then another. The wall of the diving school was starting to look like a cave painting.

Pablo shouted and cursed me in Spanish and made his way up the stairs. He was holding a bone, a yellow, stinking bone. That is what he had been reaching for under his desk.

Pablo was on the roof terrace with his bone and his dog. He was kicking a chair. The dog had stopped barking and started to snarl while Pablo made clicking sounds, which seemed to have a calming effect.

I heard a pot plant fall and shatter.

It was cool inside the diving-school reception. The phone was ringing on Pablo's desk, next to a burning coil of citronella and his glass of vermouth. An answer-machine picked up the call: 'We speak German, Dutch, English and Spanish and are able to teach beginners up to master diver.'

I lifted the glass to my cracked lips and calmly, slowly, took a tiny sip. In the new quiet I heard the sea as if my ears were laid against the ocean floor. I could hear everything. The rumbling earthquake of a ship and the spider crabs moving between weeds.

Austerity and Abundance

'Zoffie! There is going to be a massacre!'

I called Ingrid and invited her to share the dorado with me to celebrate freeing Pablo's dog. She said yes, she would come over at 9 p.m.

I showered and oiled my hair and then walked over to the plaza to buy a watermelon from the woman in the truck who I had first thought was a man. She was sitting in the driver's seat with her young grandson sprawled on her lap. They were eating figs. Purple dusty figs, the colour of twilight. She told the boy to choose me a melon, which he did, and when she took the money she put it in a cotton wallet that was strapped around the waist of her black dress. She had taken off her sandals and placed them in the compartment of the truck door. I noticed a ball of bone growing like a small island on the side of her right foot. Her arms were brown and strong, her cheek-bones sun-lashed, her hips wide as she moved to make space for her grandson when he clambered back on to her lap. Her body. Who is her body supposed to please? What is it for and is it ugly or is it something else? She silently pressed another fig into the boy's hand, resting her chin on his head. She was a farmer and grandmother running her own economy with her money bag pressed against her womb.

Ingrid Bauer walked through the open door without knocking, just as I had started to grill the dorado. She was wearing silver shorts and her silver Roman sandals were laced up her shins to just below the knee. She had painted her toenails silver, too. I showed her the table on the terrace, which I had laid for a feast. I had even found matching plates and cutlery and wine glasses. A bowl of chopped watermelon and mint was chilling in the fridge. I had made a cheesecake. Yes, this time I had baked my own bittersweet amaretto cheesecake with amaretti biscuits and sweet amaretto liqueur and the bitter peel of Seville oranges.

It was the start of a bolder life.

I offered Ingrid wine but she wanted water. I always have plenty of water ready for Rose, so it was not a problem. It was the right sort of water for Ingrid. She sat close to me.

And then closer.

'So you freed the dog?'

'Yes.'

'Did you look him in the eye?'

'No.'

'Did you give him meat?'

'No.'

'You just untied him?'

'Pablo untied him.'

'And the dog was calm and licked his leg?'

'No.'

We both knew that Pablo had been seen in the village walking his dog that afternoon. It was a catastrophe. The dog had tried to bite off the hand of a woman from Belgium when she was waiting for change at the bar. He had to be muzzled and Pablo was shouting and kicking everything in his way. Pablo needed a muzzle but he was protected by his army of cops.

'Congratulations, Zoffie!'

She gave me a gift, a yellow silk halter-neck top. She said the silk would soothe my medusa stings and she pointed to where she had sewn my initials on the left-hand corner in blue silken thread. SP. Underneath SP she had embroidered the word Beloved.

Beloved.

To be Beloved was to be something quite alien to myself. The silk sun-top smelt of her shampoo and of manuka honey and pepper. Neither of us spoke about the Beloved but we knew it was there and that her needle had authored the word. She told me she can sew on to any kind of material if she has the right needle – a shoe, a belt, even thin metal and various kinds of plastic – but it was silk she liked to work with most.

'It is alive like a bird,' she said. 'I have to catch it with my needle and make it obey me.'

Sewing was her way of keeping things together. It pleased her to mend something that seemed beyond repair. She often worked with a magnifying glass to find solutions to a rip that was hidden in the weave. The needle was the instrument she thought with, she embroidered anything that surfaced in her mind. It was a rule she had made up for herself never to censor any word or image that revealed itself to her. Today she had embroidered a snake, a star and a cigar on two shirts and on the hem of a skirt.

I asked her to repeat what she had just said.

'A snake. A star. A cigar.'

She said the idea for the word embroidered on my sun-top had been on her mind because she was thinking of her sister in Düsseldorf.

'What's your sister's name?'

'Hannah.'

'Is she older or younger?'

'I am her big, bad sister.'

'Why are you bad?'

'Ask Matty.'

'I'm asking you.'

'Okay, I'll tell you.'

She gulped down her glass of water and slammed it on the table. Tears welled in her green eyes. 'No, I won't tell you. I was talking about my sewing.'

There were apparently piles of clothes from the vintage shop waiting to be transformed with her needle. It was the same in Berlin, and she now had a contact in China who was sending her parcels of clothes to redesign. She was mostly interested in geometry, that's what she had studied at university, in Bavaria, and what she liked about the needle was its precision. Her taste was for symmetry and structure, it helped her thoughts drift. Symmetry did not chain her, it set her free. Freer than Pablo's dog would ever be.

She put her arm around my shoulders and her fingers were cold like a needle. I did not expect the weight of a word like Beloved to be delivered to me, written in blue silk with the initials of my name floating above it. She had let the word roam free, that's what she said, whatever came to her mind became the design.

Ingrid wiped her eyes with the back of her hand and told me she couldn't stay.

'Don't go, Ingrid.' I kissed her wet cheek and whispered my thanks for her precious gift. Her ears were pierced with tiny lustrous pearls.

'You are always working anyway, Zoffie. I don't want to disturb you.'

'How do you mean, I am always working?'

'Everyone is a field study to you. It makes me feel weird. Like you are watching me all the time. What is the difference between studying anthropology and practising it?'

'Well, I would get paid if I practised it.'

'That's not what I mean. Anyway, if you need some money, I can lend it to you. I have to go.'

Ingrid and Matthew were meeting friends at a tapas bar that night. Afterwards, they were going to a party in a field out of town given by a friend who was a DJ. Matthew was putting up lights there at the moment. She was supposed to have loaded bags of ice and some buckets in the car and driven them to the site but she had been embroidering my sun-top instead. The beer would still be warm by the time everyone arrived and it was sort of my fault.

'Thanks for the water, Zoffie. I need it because I'm going to be wrecked later.'

When she walked out of the open door I watched her linger for a few seconds by the table set for two on the terrace. And then she moved on to her real life.

Is this what it is like to be beloved by Ingrid Bauer?

There were two sharp knives lying on the kitchen table next to a faux ancient Greek vase. I put them away in the drawer and looked more closely at the saffron-coloured vase. It was in the shape of an urn, with a frieze drawn on it in black resin of seven slave women balancing jugs on their heads while they queued by a fountain to collect water. Obviously the vase was a copy, but it did show a historically correct event in everyday life. It was difficult to channel water into the cities of ancient Greece, so it had to be collected at public fountains. Wealthy men would drink wine mixed with the water the female slaves had carried to their homes for them, but the women had no home of their own. Tonight was the first time I had invited someone to my temporary home in Spain. It had all gone wrong when I asked about Ingrid's sister.

I turned off the heat on the dorado and found myself walking across the beach to the injury hut.

I was getting bolder.

I asked the student to join me for supper.

He looked surprised and then pleased. 'You will want to know my name is Juan,' he said.

'Yes,' I replied, 'and I will need to know your date of birth, country of origin and your occupation.'

He was stapling the day's forms together (fourteen stings recorded), but he would be with me in twenty minutes and he thanked me for the invitation. Did I know that Pablo's dog had dug up a row of sun umbrellas on the beach? Pablo's brothers had chased him, so he had run into the sea in a panic. He had swum far out and then he had disappeared. No one knew where Pablo's dog had got to or if it had drowned. If the German shepherd was still alive, the injury hut was going to have to handle a bite that was fiercer than the jellyfish. The student was laughing and scooping up his brown hair with his fingers. His neck was long and graceful.

'Pablo is saying you threatened him.'

'Yes, with the blood of the fish you are about to eat with me.'

Our eyes met and I looked at him with all the power of someone who was beloved. I knew I had been rejected by Ingrid but I left that out of what my eyes were telling him.

When he arrived he was carrying four bottles of beer, which he said he kept in the fridge in the injury hut. He asked after my mother. I told him that she was sleeping and, for once, she had not drawn the curtains to hide from 'the clapped-out stars'. We ate the dorado sitting opposite each other at the table laid for two on the terrace. Its white flesh was tender under its silver skin. He told me it was succulent because it had a layer of fat between the skin and the flesh. Later, we swam naked in the warm night and he kissed every medusa sting on my body, the welts and blisters, until I was disappointed there were not more of them. I had been stung into desire. He was my lover and I was his conqueror. It would be true to say that I was very bold.

She has ripped out my heart with her monster claws.

Bling

Rose sat limply at the wheel of the hire car while I washed the dust off the windows with a cloth. It was 11 a.m. and the sun was already burning my neck. My mother was about to drive us to a Sunday market near the airport to buy fruit and vegetables for the week. Juan had told me about a stall that sold sweet green grapes from North Africa, and I also had to find a can of coconut milk to take over to Ingrid's later, because she has invited me to make ice cream. Rose was quiet for a change and not as resentful as usual. That was my mother's main expression: slightly resentful, a whiff of resentment, not personally against me (though there was that, of course) but a vague sense of grievance against the world.

'You are always so far away, Sofia.'

I am not far away. I am always too close. To her grievances.

The medusa stings were throbbing but I liked to feel them there, just as I liked to feel the word Beloved threaded into my new silk sun-top. Beloved was the antidote to the sting. Rose had impatiently started the engine, so I threw the cloth into the bucket, hiding it under a sign that said HOTEL FAMILY. ROOMS VACANT, with an arrow pointing to a dust track that apparently led to families who had checked into Hotel Family. Simmering, fuming, seething families; monogamous, polygamous, matrilineal, patrilineal, nuclear.

We are a mother and daughter, but are we a family?

I slammed the car door.

How was my mother to drive with no feeling in her legs? But she did. She moved her feet from the clutch to the brakes to the accelerator and I just had to believe that she would not lose her grip and that I would return home unharmed to find her more of the wrong kind of water. The route to the market was a straight drive across the newly tarred motorway. Rose drove fast. She was enjoying herself, her left elbow hanging out of the window. When she asked me why I had never learned to drive, I reminded her that I had failed my driving test four times and my driving theory exam, too, and after that I'd decided to call it a day and buy a bicycle.

'Yes,' she said. 'I can't imagine you driving.'

How do we set about not imagining something? What if I said that I can't imagine human sexuality? What if I can't imagine human sexuality in a way that has not already been described to me? What if I can't imagine another culture? How would the day start and how would it end if it was beyond me to imagine Greece, the birthplace of my father? What if it is impossible to imagine he is missing his abandoned daughter and that one day we might be reconciled?

I looked down at my mother's foot on the brake. Her toes moved off and then landed on it with delicacy and confidence. 'I can imagine you walking the entire length of the beach,' I said.

In reply she started to sing the words to a hymn: 'And did those feet in ancient time/ Walk upon England's mountains green'.

If only. My mother's feet are mostly on strike, but I'm not sure what she is negotiating for or what the deal breaker would be. Her feet are an English size nine. Her jaw is large. Our ancestors developed a protruding jaw because they were constantly fighting. Grievance is very strenuous. My mother needs her jaw to see off anyone who will separate her from her stash of resentment. I need to become interested in something else because I am not earning a living to support my interest in her symptoms. I have abandoned my doctorate, which might contribute to making my interest public rather than private and earn me a licence to teach the subject that takes up all my time. Getting a licence is another one of my problems.

Rose tapped the indicator and turned right on the motorway towards the sea. 'You seem to have made some new friends here in Almería?'

I ignored her.

'There is something I should tell you about your father. Compared to my own father, he is a very gentle man.'

I could do with whatever pill she takes for dizziness but it has been deleted from the menu of her medication. My father is obviously so gentle he has not had the strength to contact me for eleven years.

Perhaps the case histories with Julieta Gómez were offering Rose another view of her former husband. She had some views of her own about Nurse Sunshine. As she sped down the motorway, she told me it was clear to her that Julieta was a drunk. Her breath often smelt of alcohol during their physiotherapy sessions. Frankly, it was a matter of ethical concern.

She was driving too fast. I was holding my breath and biting my cracked lips at the same time. 'Julieta is astute. Very clever. She is never judgemental of me, Sofia, and so I am reluctant to judge her. But it is perplexing and I will have to consider my options.'

Rose had now archived three case histories with Julieta Gómez. She had become more reflective, secretive, maybe even kinder, although she still hated the white cat, Jodo, whom she had come reluctantly to regard as a member of staff at the clinic. She wouldn't be surprised if Jodo started to administer her vitamin injections. Gómez had told her that she should draw a picture of the cat on the soles of her feet. That way she could stamp on Jodo all day long.

I thought his comment was a clever way of getting her to walk.

We parked in the driveway of an empty house on the edge of the motorway. A pile of abandoned, torn clothes was strewn across the porch. As I lifted the wheelchair out of the boot I could see the sprawl of the market across the road. An aeroplane flew low in the sky, preparing to land at the nearby airport. It is such hard work carrying my mother. In she goes. I am pushing her across the hot tarmac towards a stall that has a few tables and chairs laid out in the shade. Rose demanded I queue up for a portion of churros, which she would enjoy with a small glass of anise liqueur. She even finished her request with 'Thank you, Fia.'

We are in a lunar landscape. That's what all the guides say about Almería. Wind-beaten and sun-baked. The riverbeds are cracked and dry. A blue petrol haze floats above the tattered stalls selling handbags and purple grapes and onions. I wheel Rose to some shade under the plastic awning held up by rusty poles. Already she is talking to an elderly man who is sitting with a bandage around his right knee. They seem to be having a conversation about walking sticks.

The churros come in two shapes, long sausages to dip into chocolate and then a shorter kind. I buy us the longer ones and carry Rose her anise liqueur in a paper cup.

The old man is waving his walking stick in the air and showing my mother the rubber tip on the end of it. I sit down next to them and pretend to be fascinated by the rubber tip.

I am in a reckless mood after my bold night of lovemaking under the real night stars. I want to sit here with a lover, close, closer, touching. Instead I am here with my mother, who is a sort of career invalid. I am young and might even be the subject of erotic dreams newly minted by Juan, who had said, 'The dream is over,' when we first met. And I might be beloved to Ingrid, who is tormenting me.

Rose taps my hand. 'Fia, I would like to buy a watch.'

I shoved a churro in my mouth. It was crisp and oily and sprinkled with sugar. No wonder my body was shape-shifting towards the east and west while I lived in Spain.

Rose's breath was hot from the anise. She seemed to be able to swallow fiery licorice liqueur more easily than she could swallow water. 'By the way, if you can work those complicated coffee machines, believe me, you can drive a car. It's really very easy to drive.' When she tipped her head back and slurped the anise in one go, I thought she was going to gargle with it.

At that moment, my real mother and my ghostly mother – the woman who is glorious, victorious, well and vital – morphed together. That was another good subject for an original field study – the way imagination and reality tumble together and mess things up – but I was too distracted by the woman wearing one of the more flamboyant straw hats displayed on her stall to think about it. The price label was still attached to the hat with a string, so it kept swinging across her eyes. It was as if she had put something in the way of being looked at. Every now and again she jerked her head to make the label swing chaotically across her face.

I stood up and took my place behind the wheelchair, lifted up the brake, which was difficult because my espadrilles were flopping off my feet, and began to push my mother down the dust road, dodging the potholes and dog shit, past the handbags and purses, the sweating cheeses and gnarled salamis, the jamón ibérico from Salamanca, the strings of chorizo, plastic tablecloths and mobile-phone covers, the chickens turning on a stainless-steel spit, the cherries, bruised apples, oranges and peppers, the couscous and turmeric heaped in baskets, the jars of harissa and preserved lemons, the torches, spanners, hammers, while Rose swatted the flies landing on her feet with a rolled-up copy of the *London Review of Books*.

I paused on the dust road.

My mother can feel a fly landing on her feet.

A fly. She can feel a fly.

She is not numb. She is acutely sensitive.

As I resumed pushing her along, I could still hear the swish of her literary fly-swat as I gazed out at the unhomely grey-concrete apartment blocks that were now abandoned in the recession.

'Stop Stop Stop.'

Rose was pointing at a stall of cheap watches. A tall African man in an elegant white robe waved to her with his left hand. Draped across his right arm which he had curved into the shape of a C was an array of headphones: blue, red and white headphones. Rose shouted to me to move her chair closer and immediately grabbed a bright gold metal watch with a thick wristband, its face studded with a circle of fake diamonds.

'I have always wanted a gangster watch. This is the bling to see me out.'

'To see you out of what?'

'I am slowly being murdered at the Gómez Clinic, Sofia. My medication is dwindling and the staff at the clinic have no diagnostic skills whatsoever. They tell me everything is in order. Do I look like I am thriving?' She slammed her feet on the wheelchair. 'So far, what with the foot ulcers, it looks like diabetes. It's the only thing that quack and his cat are taking seriously.'

The African man gently freed the watch from my mother's fingers and started to fiddle with the winder. He held the diamond-studded face against his ear and shook it. Obviously, he didn't like what he heard. He dipped his hand into the pocket of his white robe and took out a small screwdriver. By the time he was taking it apart I knew Rose was going to have to buy it.

I stepped in front of her. 'How much is that watch?' I had placed my hands on my hips as if I was indignant, which I was not. That was odd. I was imitating indignation, but my heart wasn't in it. Where did I learn to express indignation I did not feel, my voice veering up the scales to land on a note which could be described as accusing? Where did I learn to adopt an attitude that I do not believe in? And what about the word Beloved? Perhaps Ingrid was imitating something she did not feel when she embroidered that word in blue thread and gave it to me as if it were of no importance.

He told me the watch was only fifty euro.

I started to laugh, but sarcasm is not the same as laughing and he knew it.

Now he was delicately holding a tiny round disc of steel between his long fingers. Rose explained to me that it was a battery, as if this were an entirely new invention.

They both became very involved in the battery. He was nodding and smiling in agreement with her, pointing to the diamonds as if they were priceless. The anise liqueur had flushed Rose's cheeks. When she started counting the number of diamonds in the circle, he understood that her wrist would not be naked for much longer. I realized my mother had charm and verve. If I blew on her name, ROSE, the letters would shuffle around and come out as EROS, the god of love, winged but lame.

She held out her wrist and the man attached the watch around it.

I could see it was too big for her small bones and always would be. He dragged a stool to the side of her wheelchair and invited her to rest her wrist on his knee while he fiddled with the links of the gold band. The hairs on her arm were trapped under the links. I found myself wincing as if I were feeling this small pain on her behalf. Empathy is more painful than medusa stings.

While my mother proceeded with the ritual of purchasing a time-keeping device to 'see her out', I walked to a stall selling brooms and mousetraps, among other things. An abundance of pink and blue birthday-cake candles were laid out on foil trays. Three candles for one euro. The more expensive ones were silver and had matching spiked silver holders to pierce the cake. I gazed at a variety of mops and buckets, pots and pans, wooden spoons and sieves. I have never had a home of my own in my adult life so far. If I made a home, what would I buy from this stall of domestic goods? I would apparently have moths and mice to kill and rats and flies. I picked up an aerosol of air freshener that had been designed in the shape of a curvaceous woman. She was wearing a polka-dot apron that did not disguise her massive belly and heavy breasts. Her eyelashes were long and curled, her lips tiny and puckered. The instructions for how to use her were translated into Italian, Greek, German, Danish and a language I did not recognize, but she was 'Extremely Flammable' in every language.

There were instructions in English, too. Shake her well. Point her towards the centre of the room and spray. The scale of her belly and breasts was not unlike early fertility goddesses found in Greece around 6000 BC, except they did not wear polka-dot aprons. Did they suffer from hypochondria? Hysteria? Were they bold? Lame? Too full of the milk of human kindness?

I bought the air freshener for four euro because it was a kind of artefact translated into many languages, and also because it was clearly an interpretation of a woman (breasts belly apron eyelashes) and I had become confused by the signs for *servicios* in public places. I could not figure out why one sign was male and the other female. The most common stick-figure sign was not particularly male or female. Did I need this aerosol to make things clearer to me? What kind of clarity was I after?

I had conquered Juan who was Zeus the thunderer as far as I was concerned, but the signs were all mixed up because his job in the injury hut was to tend the wounded with his tube of ointment. He was maternal, brotherly, he was like a sister, perhaps paternal, he had become my lover. Are we all lurking in each other's sign? Do I and the woman on the air freshener belong to the same sign? Another aeroplane was flying above the market, its metal body heavy in the sky. A male pilot I had met in the Coffee House had told me that an aircraft was always referred to as 'she'. His task was to keep her in balance, to make her an extension of his hands, to make her responsive to the lightest of touch. She was sensitive and needed to be handled delicately. A week later, after we had slept together, I discovered that he was also responsive to the lightest of touch.

It wasn't clarity I was after. I wanted things to be less clear.

The African man and my mother seemed to be hitting it off. He was telling her about the history of Almería while he took the watch off her wrist so she could soothe the fine hair that had been caught in the links. He was taking a long time to sell her that watch.

' "Almería" in Arabic means "the mirror of the sea".'

Rose was pretending to listen but all her attention was on her diamond-studded watch. 'It's ticking! I can feel the ticking because my arms are not numb like my feet.'

It is a time-keeping device to see her out and it is ticking.

'I have difficulty walking,' Rose told the African salesman. He shook his head in commercial sympathy as she waved a fifty-euro note in the air with a flourish and then graciously passed it to him. 'Thank you for your time.'

He waved us goodbye as the sun warmed the brine in the bucket of olives and giant capers nearby. Everything smelt of harsh, dark vinegar.

'Do you want to know the time, Sofia?'

'Oh Yes Please.'

'It is twelve forty-five. Time for my dwindling medication.'

When we arrive back at the car I invite Rose to get out of her wheelchair and stand while I fold and stack it in the boot.

'It's not a matter of will, Sofia. I can't stand today.'

By the time I had heaved my mother into the car, her groans, moans, hisses and then insults all directed at me, and then my flaws, imperfections and irritating habits, I felt that she was indeed a gangster and that she was mugging my life.

I sat down on the passenger seat, slammed the door and waited for her to drive us away, but she had become very still, as if she was in shock. We had parked outside the ruin of a house that we thought was uninhabited. But now we saw that people were living there despite the holes in the roof and broken windows. A mother and her young daughter were eating soup on the porch. Everything was broken, the wheelbarrow, the pram, the chairs, the table and the doll with one arm that was lying near the car.

It was a broken home in every sense.

My mother was the head of her own small, broken family.

It was her responsibility to stop wild animals sneaking in through the door and terrifying her child. It was as if this sad house was a spectre she carried inside her, the fear of not keeping the wolf from our door in Hackney, London. I had been entitled to free school meals at my school and Rose knew I was ashamed. She had made me soup in a flask most days before she left for work. I carried it in my heavy schoolbag while it leaked all over my homework. That flask of soup was a torment but it was proof to my mother that the wolf had not yet arrived. My guidebook has a whole page on the Iberian wolves (*Canis lupus signatus*) that once flourished in Almería. Apparently, during Franco's dictatorship, there was a special campaign to exterminate the wolves. Obviously some of them had survived and hadn't bothered to knock on the door of this house. They had crashed through the windows.

An aeroplane cut a white trail in the sky.

The child waved her spoon at my mother.

'Sofia, drive us home.' Rose threw the keys into my lap.

'I can't drive.'

'Yes, you can. Anyway, that anise liqueur was too strong and I can't drive either.'

She started to edge her body into the passenger seat so I had to jump out of the car. I walked round to the driver's seat, sat down, inserted the key into the ignition. The engine started. I fiddled with the handbrake and began to reverse.

'That's perfect,' Rose said. 'A perfect reverse.'

Something crunched under the wheels.

'It's that poor child's doll,' my mother said, peering out of the window. 'Never mind, change gear, indicator on, put your seat belt on, very good, off we go.'

I was driving at ten miles an hour while Rose leaned forward to adjust the mirror. 'Faster.'

I was in the wrong gear but then I corrected the gear stick's position and even dared to increase the speed along the new, empty motorway.

'Sofia, I feel completely safe in your hands. Just one observation.'

'What?'

'In Spain, you drive on the right-hand side of the road.'

I laughed and Rose told me the time on her new watch.

'We are going uphill, so you need to change gear. Can you see there is a car trying to overtake us?'

'Yes, I can see him.'

'It's a her,' she said. 'A her is trying to overtake you because she has perfect visibility, she can see there are no vehicles coming in her direction. It's one o'clock, by the way.'

Driving was a breeze after working the coffee machines, just as Rose said it would be.

Something was rolling around in the boot. Every time I turned a corner it banged against the sides. I slowed down and the car suddenly jerked and stopped.

'You have to find a better balance between the brake and the accelerator. Into neutral and start again.'

The Berlingo lurched forward and the object in the boot rattled around.

'That is not neutral.' Rose adjusted the gears for me and we were off. 'It is not your lack of a licence that worries me, it is your lack of spectacles. I will have to be your eyes.'

She is my eyes. I am her legs.

After we arrived in the car park at the end of the village and I had pulled up the handbrake, Rose announced she had a new chauffeur.

My love for my mother is like an axe. It cuts very deep.

She stretched out her finger to touch the oiled curls on the nape of my neck. 'I'm not sure what you're doing to your hair, Fia. You remind me of the taxi driver who got lost taking your father and myself to our hotel in Kefalonia for our honeymoon.'

She gestured to me to pass her the keys. 'Your father was very proud of his hair, and I was forbidden to touch it. In those days his hair was long and fell to his shoulders in soft black curls. In the end, I began to regard it as symbolic hair.'

I did not want to know any of this. But as she had told Gómez, I was her only.

When I opened the door for her in my new role as chauffeur, she told me she would walk home. Walking was, apparently, no problem at all. I turned my back on her and searched the boot for the object that had been rattling around. When I eventually found it, I guessed that Matthew must have hidden it in the boot after he picked up the hire car and signed off the papers with Nurse Sunshine.

It was an aerosol of blue spray-paint.

Rose was leaning against the trunk of the palm tree at the end of the car park. She was bent over as if carrying something too heavy to bear.

Horseplay

The Kiss. We don't talk about it but it's there in the coconut ice cream we are making together. It's there in the space between us as Ingrid scrapes the seeds from a vanilla pod with her penknife. It's lurking in her long eyelids and in the egg yolks and cream and it's written in blue silken thread with the needle that is Ingrid's mind. I don't know what I want from Ingrid or why she enjoys humiliating me or why I put up with it.

It seems that I have consented to being undermined.

She shows me the clothes piled in baskets all over the floor of their Spanish house and pulls out a white satin dress with thin, fraying straps. It has a stain on the hem but she says it would suit me. She'll mend it when she gets round to it because she knows my medusa stings hurt all the time.

They don't hurt all the time but I don't want to disappoint her. While we wait for the ice cream to set in the freezer she twists a strand of my hair around her finger. 'Let me cut out this knot,' she says.

She reaches for a pair of ornate, sharp scissors lying on top of one of the baskets of clothes. The blades saw through my hair. When I turn round she is holding a thick strand of my curls like a trophy in her hand. I feel uneasy but it is more exciting than waiting for my mother's side effects and withdrawal symptoms. Perhaps feeling uneasy is a side effect?

'Zoffie, do anthropologists steal heads from graves to measure and classify them?'

'No, that was in the old days. I'm not looking for heads in graves.'

'What are you looking for, then?'

'Nothing.'

'Really, Zoffie?'

Yes.

'Why is nothing interesting?'

'Because it covers up everything.'

She punched my arm. 'You spend too much time on your own. You should make something with your hands.'

'Like what?'

'A bridge.'

If Ingrid is a bridge leading me across the swamp beneath it, she keeps taking a few of the bricks out every time we meet. It is like an erotic rite of passage. If I manage to cross the bridge without falling into the swamp, perhaps I will be compensated for my suffering? Ingrid's lips are luscious, soft and full. She is poised, a woman of few words, but the word she has chosen, Beloved, is a big word.

She commands me to sit in the garden with Matthew who has just returned from work.

He is lying in a hammock slung between two trees in the shade. 'To-day was an ex-per-i-ence.' Matthew pushes his foot against the tree and the hammock starts to sway from left to right. 'The hardest thing, Sophie, is to get people to be themselves.'

He waves his hands at the leaves above his head, as if conjuring a self that might be true enough for him.

It turns out that Matthew is a life coach. He teaches senior managers to communicate better, to sell their brand and put it across with humour and vigour.

Is Matthew being himself?

He is friendly but shifty, and I don't blame him because his girlfriend is messing with me and he's messing with something too, but

I'm not sure what's going on. Something like his right hand wrote a blue message to Julieta Gómez while his left hand caressed Ingrid Bauer's long, tanned thighs.

Ingrid carries out a tray of her home-made lemonade, a pair of silver tongs, a sprig of fresh mint and a jug of ice. After she has formally kissed Matthew on his cheek, she fills a plastic glass with ice and then pours the lemonade, adding a slice of lime and a few leaves of mint. She is not exactly a wife. More like a cocktail waitress who is also an athlete and a mathematician. She has studied geometry and she is a seamstress with clients in China. She is also 'a big, bad sister', but she doesn't want to talk about that.

Matthew's hobby is collecting wine. He has gone on a few courses taught by the masters, the buyers and sommeliers who focus on a particular grape, or a region where the grapes are grown. Here in Spain he has found a fellow wine expert, a horse-riding instructor called Leonardo who owns a cortigo – a country house with its own stables. Ingrid rents one of the rooms there in order to sew. She works on Tuesdays and Wednesdays – just two days because life is short – and Matthew, who is also short, misses her when she is away from him.

'Zoffie, perhaps you would like to see the cortigo? My machines are old, from India. I bought them on eBay and they have never broken down. They are heavy, really beautiful objects.'

Matthew looks bored, so she starts to talk about him. He finds himself very lovable and Ingrid seems to love him. He is radiant with self-belief.

Everything I know about myself is cracking and Ingrid is the hammer.

Matthew insists she sits in the shade. She ignores him and sits in the sunshine by my side.

He lifts up his head and smiles at me, as if we both share an interest in Ingrid's well-being. 'Tell Inge to move out of the sun. She's got pale skin, so it's not healthy.'

I shake my curls at him. 'Sunshine is sexy.'

Matthew scoops out a mint leaf from his glass and begins to chew on it. 'That's a tricky one, Sophie. There are debates in the scientific community about sunshine. It warms the planet every day, but it also makes us blind.'

'Blind to what?'

'Our everyday responsibilities. It is very seductive.'

While we are on the subject of responsibilities, he wants to know about my mother. 'So did you pay a lot of money to the Gómez Clinic?'

'Yes.'

He tucks his blond hair behind his ears and nods, as if he knows this already. 'Look, Sophie, I can tell you, that so-called "doctor" should be struck off.'

'You might be right.'

'I *am* right. Gómez is dangerous and he's an arsehole.'

'How do you know?'

'I'm training an executive from Los Angeles here in Spain at the moment. He says Gómez is a discredited quack.'

While we talk, Ingrid is placing a few small pebbles around a potted baby cactus which she has balanced on her lap. 'Zoffie is just trying to help her mother and your client is unreliable.'

Matthew shakes his head s-l-o-w-ly as the hammock creaks and sways. 'No, he is not unreliable. Tony James is a great guy. Today I did an exercise with him where he throws a golf ball up in the air and catches it while he speaks. He stopped being a zombie. It was like seeing traffic lights change.' He reaches for the leaves above his head and touches them with his fingertips.

I have to become bolder. I have to find more courage and purpose and chase my thoughts. 'Does Tony James work for a pharmaceutical company?'

Matthew tosses his empty glass of lemonade on to the ground. 'Yuh.'

The cicadas have started their call for the afternoon.

Yuh is a good subject for an original field study.

Yuh has covered the subject of the pharmaceutical company in the white plastic that covers the tomatoes and peppers growing in desert sweat farms. And Matthew has covered the marble wall of the Gómez Clinic with the words 'Sunshine is Sexy'. Yet he seems to be angry with Julieta Gómez.

I'm not sure I believe he is authentically in love with Ingrid.

After a while I tell him I like his red leather belt.

'Thank you. I like it because Ingrid bought it for me.' He sounds relieved to be back on track.

Anthropologists have to veer off track, otherwise we would never rearrange our own belief systems. There would be no one to throw water at our smokescreens. No one to tell us that our reality is incompatible with other realities or to understand the significance of the plan of a village and its dwellings – its relationship to life and death, or why the women live on the periphery of the village.

Matthew continues on his track. He adjusts his position in the hammock and starts to swing with new force as he explains how he has developed a method to help his clients, mostly from oil companies, give their PowerPoint presentations. It is his job to help them project who they are and what they value, to learn how to stand with authority and confidence and not to worry about cracking a few jokes to get the audience onside. He has forbidden them to use phrases like 'The tail is wagging the dog' or 'You are a star.' CEOs always stumble with their autocue technique and so he gives them strategies to cope with stumbling, to make something of it rather than pretending it hasn't happened. He finds it very rewarding to help free up the leadership potential in his clients. When they reveal their frailties about performing in public or being disliked by their staff, the feeling between his clients and himself is something like love. He encourages them to develop their eccentricities. Yesterday, he told Mr James from Los Angeles to take the golf ball with him to all meetings. Throwing it around while he talks will become his signature gesture.

Matthew stretches out his arms on either side of the hammock to suggest he is flying. The odd thing is that I heard a trace of some of the things Julieta Gómez had implied with fewer words when she recorded my mother's case history, except they were altered when they came out of Matthew's mouth. It was as if he had hijacked something she did and applied it to what he did. The executives he trains are his sacred buffalo. He helps them build a persona, a mask through which they can speak authentically on behalf of the brand. The face beneath the mask has to grow seamlessly into the mask. If this apparatus cracks they can call upon him to put it together again.

Ingrid walks into the shade and stands under the tree. I notice for the first time that her belly button is pierced with a green jewel in the shape of a tear. There are spines from the cactus in her fingers and she wants Matthew to pull them out for her.

'Hey, keep out of the way of my hammock, Inge.' He sounds vaguely threatening.

She waves her spiked fingers above his face. 'Matty, you should shut up.' She points to her lips and makes a zipping gesture. 'Everything is a field study to Zoffie. She is taking notes. Believe me, she will give a paper on your life-coaching methods and then everyone will know your secrets.'

'Keep your distance, Inge. This is my hammock and I don't need a push.' It is as if he is chastising her for something.

She walks back into the shade and places her hand on my knee. 'Then Zoffie will take out the needles.'

'So what's your job, Sophie?' Matthew speaks over her, his eyes now closed as he sways gently under the leaves.

'I make artisan coffee.'

'That's a good skill. How do you make it perfect?'

'Quality beans, texture of the grind, the way the water flows through the coffee.'

He nods gravely, as if we were discussing something important. 'So what do you want?'

'How do you mean?'

'You know, insane things like work, money, being included in the game? If you had to write your wish list and you could use invisible ink, what would it be?'

I can see my face flushing in the various triangle-shaped shards of mirror that have been planted around the desert plants in their garden.

'Zoffie has nothing on her wish list. Nothing nothing nothing.' Ingrid flutters her spiked fingertips on my knee.

I am deformed with embarrassment. Have I ever said what I meant in my life so far? So why would I say it to Matthew?

He snaps his fingers and laughs. 'You need an autocue, Sophie! That's what Julieta Gómez does, isn't it? She prompts her clients to jog their memory?'

I stand up and jump over the low stone wall that separates their garden from the beach. One of the good things happening to me here in Spain is that I now jump over things.

I am so lonely.

I am walking on the sand and the tide is out. A woman is galloping on her horse across the burning sand of the playa. A tall Andalusian horse. His mane is flaming his hooves are thundering the sea is glittering. She is wearing blue velvet shorts and brown riding boots and she is holding a giant bow and arrow. Her upper arms are muscled, her long hair is braided, she is gripping the horse with her thighs. I can hear her breathing as the arrow flies through the air and enters my heart. I am wounded. I am wounded with desire and I am ready for the ordeal of love.

Four boys are playing volleyball on the beach, thumping the ball over the net. When the ball comes towards me I jump high and whack it back to them. They cheer and wave to me.

One of them was Juan.

Ingrid and Juan. He is masculine and she is feminine but, like a deep perfume, the notes cut into each other and mingle.

When the Greek girl speaks her accent is English but her hair is black like the bread my father eats with salted lard and mustard. In the morning she saves watermelon rinds for the chickens that live in the yard near the cemetery at the back of the village. She puts the rinds in a carrier bag every morning and takes them to Señora Bedello who owns the chickens. The wide brim of her sombrero casts a shadow around her shoulders. Her medusa stings are fading.

Human Shields

There was a strange atmosphere in the consulting room. Gómez looked irritated. His shirtsleeves were rolled up and the alarming white streak in his hair was damp with sweat.

'I am not so sure how to read this most recent X-ray. There is no doubt that you, Rose, are losing bone density, but this is normal in women who are aged fifty and older.' He sighed and folded his arms across his pinstripes. 'Bone is very interesting. It is made from collagen and minerals. It is a living tissue. After the age of forty-five all of our bones become less dense and less strong. Yet you have not suffered from a significant loss of bone material. I suggest you walk home.'

The single silver hair on my mother's chin stood erect.

'Mrs Papastergiadis, if you want to continue with the treatment you will have to give up all your medication. All of it. Every single pill. For high cholesterol, for sleeping, for heart palpitations, for indigestion, for migraines, for back pains, for blood-pressure regulation and all the painkillers. Everything.'

To my surprise, Rose looked straight into his eyes and agreed to his request. 'I am ready to start working with you, Mr Gómez.'

Gómez obviously did not believe her either. He clapped his hands. 'But I have good news! My true love is pregnant!'

At first I did not know what he meant, but then I understood that he was referring to the white cat. He walked over to me and gave me his arm. It was an invitation to link my arm in his. Bone to bone with all our densities and holes covered by skin and clothes, he guided me out of his consulting room like a bride, across the marble floor to a small alcove by the pillars.

A cardboard box had been placed in the shadow. Jodo was lying inside it on a sheepskin rug. When she saw Gómez she narrowed her eyes and started to lick her milky paws. He knelt down and stroked her under the chin until Jodo's intense, deep purring overwhelmed every other sound in the marble dome of the clinic. I realized for the first time that the ceilings were low. In some ways its architecture resembled a tent stretched out in the scorched desert.

'The vet tells me she is six weeks pregnant and so she has another three weeks to go.' He pointed to her belly. 'Can you see the bulge? Really, I was sentimental when I gave her this sheepskin. It will have to go. The soft thing she lies on must not have a scent because the mother and the kittens recognize each other by smell.'

He was much more interested in his white cat than in my mother. Perhaps the white streak in his hair had enhanced their affinity? I refused to kneel down with him to worship fat, white Jodo.

'Your lips are moving, Sofia Irina,' he said. 'It's as if your tongue is simmering inside your mouth.'

I wanted him to reassure me that it was safe for my mother to come off all her medication, but I was not bold enough to ask.

'You work in the field of anthropology. Give me three words that come to mind from your education.'

' "Archaic". "Residual". "Pre-emergent".'

'They are powerful words. They could probably make me pregnant if I thought hard enough about them.'

I raised my eyebrow, imitating Ingrid's expression when she was bewildered.

'One other matter. I understand you are driving the hire car which is in your mother's name.'

'Yes.'

'I assume you are in possession of a driving licence?'

Something was bleeping in the right pocket of Gómez's trousers, but he didn't seem to notice. 'You have become used to administering your mother's medication. So perhaps it is as if you are coming off medication, too? You are using your mother like a shield to protect yourself from making a life. Medication is a ritual which I have now erased from both your lives. Attention! You will have to invent another one.'

The dark blue circles outlining his pale blue eyes resembled the charm in the shape of a blue eye that my father used to carry with him at all times.

'Sofia Irina, listen to my bleeper! I have loved it ever since I was a junior doctor. Only the real emergencies get through. But I know its days are numbered. Nurse Sunshine wants me to change to another device.'

It was still bleeping while he traced his fingers around the bulge in the cat's white fur. After a while, he took it out of his pocket and glanced at it. 'I thought so. A heart attack in Vera, south-east of Huércal. There is not one single tree growing there, unlike in Taberno, with its beautiful orange trees. But I cannot answer this call, because I am not a cardiologist.' He switched the bleeper off and slipped it back into his pocket.

She is standing naked in her bedroom. Her breasts are full and firm. And now she is jumping. She is jumping with her arms stretched out like an aeroplane. She does not shave her armpits. What is she doing? Star jumps. Six seven eight. Her nipples are darker than her skin. She saw me in the mirror on her wall. Her eyes flickered to the left, she put her hand over her mouth. She has no one to tell her to close the blinds.

The Artist

Julieta Gómez had given me directions to her studio. It was near a small park in Carboneras, so she told me to leave the car in a side street and walk from there. I was driving the Berlingo all the time now. It was easy, apart from getting the gear into neutral, but that wasn't the biggest problem in my life. My main fear was being stopped by the police and not having the right documents. This was another similarity I shared with the unpaid Mexicans who Pablo had sacked, and the immigrants working in the furnace of the desert farms.

Do you have a licence?

Yuh.

In the style of the old colonial anthropologists, I would slip the *guardia civil tráfico* thirteen glass beads and three mother-of-pearl river shells. If that wasn't enough, I would give him a parcel of fish hooks from Bolivia, and if he wanted more I would offer two eggs from Señora Bedello's hens to slip into his khaki pocket next to his revolver. I don't know what I would do. I reversed into a parking space between a car and three bins and knocked over all the bins.

Twelve schoolgirls were having a dancing lesson on a wooden stage in the park which was circled by wilting lemon trees. They all wore brightly coloured flamenco dresses and matching dancing shoes, their hair scraped into tight, stern buns. I watched them clicking their fingers and stamping their heels. They tried not to smile but some of them couldn't help it. They were about nine years old. Will they get their driving licence, as I never did, and all the other licences they need to function on Earth? Will they be fluent in multiple languages and will they have lovers, some of them female, some of them male, and will they survive the earthquakes, floods and droughts of a changing climate and will they slip a coin into the supermarket-trolley slot to search the aisles for tomatoes and courgettes grown in the furnace of the slave farms?

A bulge of purple bougainvillea was growing over the wall of the industrial building that turned out to be Julieta Gómez's studio. It was the last of three small warehouses at the end of a cobblestoned mews. I pressed the bell next to her name.

She opened the metal door and led me to an empty room that smelt of oil paint and turpentine. Today, she wore jeans and a T-shirt and trainers, but her eyes were lined with a perfect flick at the end and her nails painted red. The floor was concrete, the walls bare brick and leaning against them were six paintings and a few blank linen canvases. Apart from a leather sofa, three wooden chairs and the fridge, there was no other furniture, and certainly none of the things I had seen on the market stall to make a home. Not even a mouse- moth- rat- or fly-trap. There were glasses and cups and two breadboards on the table. The shelves were crammed with books.

Julieta told me how to pronounce her name.

'Whoolieta.'

She explained that her full name is Gómez Peña. The reason her father calls her Nurse Sunshine is because her mother died when she was a teenager and she never smiled. 'It sort of works, and it cheers up the patients.' She passed me a beer from the fridge and took one for herself.

I told her that I have often wanted to change my surname because no one knows how to pronounce it. Not one day has gone by in my life without someone asking me how to pronounce the letters after 'Papa' in 'Papastergiadis'.

'But you haven't changed your name, so perhaps it interests you?'
She lifted the beer to her lips and took a long swig. 'This is what I do
in my spare time.'

Does she mean she drinks in her spare time?

She walked towards the wall and turned a canvas around to reveal
a painting. It was a portrait of a young woman in a traditional black
Spanish dress. She had startling, bulging, round eyes. Oily eyes like
a fly, except bigger, the size of a two-euro coin. She was holding a
fan under her chin and she looked a bit like Julieta.

'That's me with the eyes of a chameleon.' The real Julieta laughed
at the long silence that disguised my horror. 'One is not born a chameleon, one becomes one.'

I wondered if she was drunk.

'So do you like animals?'

I sounded totally dumb, but I didn't know what to say about her
nightmare eyes.

'Yes. I like to live with animals. So does my father.'

Julieta told me that when she was a child she used to have a cocker
spaniel but spaniels get dognapped in this part of Spain. The neigh-
bours had seen a Toyota truck pull up in the early hours and her dog
disappeared. Her mother had been an engineer. She had designed an
inland pipe system to transport water from rivers in the more fertile
parts of Andalucía to the desert. She had died in a helicopter crash on
the Sierra Nevada and her father had to identify her body in the hospital in Granada. It was the second disappearance in Julieta's life and
sometimes she got mixed up in her dreams so it was her mother who
was stolen in the Toyota truck.

I asked her where she had learned her interviewing techniques for
what she called my mother's 'case histories'.

'Oh, I do all the archiving for the clinic, because I speak good
English.' She pressed the toe of her trainer into the concrete floor as
if she were stubbing out a cigarette.

When I looked down I saw that she had stamped on a cockroach.

'So why is a case history called physiotherapy?' I was looking at her more searchingly now that I had seen her self-portrait.

She sat on the big cracked leather sofa and crossed her legs, beer bottle in her hand. 'Please sit.' She gestured to one of the three wooden chairs near the table.

I pulled it nearer to the sofa and sat down. The studio was light and cool. I liked being there with her, drinking beer and talking. I felt calmer than I'd felt for a long time. Calm like a bird floating tranquilly in the sea, surrendering to the waves and currents. I felt at ease with myself, which must have meant that she did not regard me as strange and so I had no reason to imitate someone who was less strange and had been saved from doing the chameleon thing.

Perhaps I was drunk, too.

She sipped her beer and asked me if I liked this particular brand. She preferred Estrella, but this was San Miguel.

I did like it.

'Physiotherapy is a major part of what we do at the clinic. My father has his strategies and procedures. At the same time, of course, he has been looking for diagnostic clues for your mother's symptoms. He has measured electrical activity in the muscles and the brain, but there is nothing to suggest concern. He does not believe he has missed an obscure organic illness or a vascular disease.'

'Yes,' I said, 'but I was asking you about the case histories.'

'It is best, Sofia, not to mistake her paralysis for physical fragility.'

'That is why we are here in Spain. To find out if there is a physical problem.' I was getting bolder.

She looked up at me, and she was smiling. I was smiling too.

Perhaps we were imitating each other's smile and doing the chameleon thing?

Except her teeth were blindingly white and mostly made from porcelain. They were perfect. I don't know why perfect is weird, but it is. I sometimes wonder about porcelain veneers. What if they fall off to expose the teeth beneath them that have been filed to a pointy stump, like a monster's teeth?

Julieta leaned her head back on the sofa and glanced at the black stain on the toe of her trainers. 'The archiving is the more interesting part of my job. I did not want to study the sciences, but I obeyed my father and took up a clinical placement in Barcelona. I was very bored every day. They wanted me to specialize in post-operation bleeds. Disaster!'

'So why didn't you go to art school?'

'I have no talent. But I suggested the clinic should be built from marble to celebrate my deceased mother's pale skin.'

We were sort of twins. One of us motherless, the other fatherless.

It was exciting to talk to Julieta in her studio. She told me she lived elsewhere, but the recession had given her the opportunity to buy a share of this property, which used to be a sardine-packing warehouse. I began to see that she was formidable. When I first met her she was so groomed and stylish that I doubted she was effective. But what did I want a nurse or physiotherapist to look like? Her problems with her father were reassuring because I had problems with my father and she was interested in the thesis I was writing for my doctorate. I found myself talking to her about its themes, which are to do with cultural memory. I told her how I felt guilty when things went right for me, as if the things going right were responsible for the things that went wrong for my mother.

'Rose will be the first to tell you that guilt is very disabling.' Julieta pointed to the ceiling. A spider had built an intricate web between the beams and had just caught a wasp in its silken trap.

I sipped my beer and told her how hard it was to return to the temporary beach house in Spain to live with my mother after her medication had been cancelled, but that I had nowhere else to go. I am always living in someone else's home.

I talked for a long time.

The spider hadn't moved from her place in the web and neither had the wasp.

I have no grip on time any more.

Julieta Gómez was now the holder of secrets, some of my own, but mostly my mother's confessed childhood. If Rose's bones were the medical subjects, the skeletons in the cupboard were another sort of subject. Everything that was transmitted from generation to generation was there in Julieta's audio archive. I asked Julieta again why she called this process physiotherapy. Is it because my mother's memories are held in her bones and muscles?

'Well, Sofia, you are the expert on this because you are writing your thesis on cultural memory.'

We talked for over an hour and I began to wonder if there was a recording device in her studio. I was nervous I had revealed too much, but she had revealed something about herself because she had got through another two bottles of beer during our conversation. All the same, I had started to think of her as a role model – except I would not be able to rise to the cut of her clothes, to her designer shoes or her vigorous intake of beer – and, not least, to the skill of her interviewing technique. She was silent for the rest of our conversation, yet she was not passive. I was thinking about the flaws in my own interviewing style when I heard a motorbike engine revving outside her studio. There had been one particular informant who had become disorientated when I interrupted him. I had spoken over him and in the end he just walked away. Now, someone was shouting through the letterbox of Julieta's front door. The door was being pushed open, the metal scraping against the concrete floor and then it slammed shut.

Matthew walked into the studio carrying a bottle of wine. When he saw me sitting on the chair his head jerked as if someone had just pronged his cheek with a fork. He tried to arrange his face into an expression that was neutral, which is the gear in the Berlingo that always gives me the most trouble. He wasn't doing very well either.

'Oh, hi, Sophie,' he said. He glanced at Julieta on the sofa and then tipped his head to the side so his hair fell over his eyes. 'I'm just calling round to give your mother's nurse a bottle of wine from my cellar.' Julieta parted her lips to show her blinding teeth. 'No, Matthew, no. Never walk through my door without knocking first. There is a bell with my name beside it on the door.' She turned her gaze to me. 'Matthew thinks he can walk in while I am working,' she said. 'For some reason, he thinks he can shout through the letterbox and do what he likes. So now I need to be alone with him to teach him some manners.'

Matthew's attention was now firmly fixed on the squashed cockroach on the floor.

'It's a bit of a tricky one.'

Julieta stood up and pointed at him with her red fingernails. 'Well, are you my patient, or are you just calling round with some wine? It's not so strange to wish to seduce your physiotherapist, but to spray this wish on the walls of her father's workplace like a cat sprays its urine is insane.'

I wondered if she had used the word 'insane' in the same way Matthew always used it, or whether she meant it? He had looked a bit crazed in the hammock when he had stretched out his arms like a corporate messiah.

'Yeah, right.' Matthew shook his hair out of his eyes and raised his thumb in my direction. 'Julieta thinks I'm a cat. They're really into animals at the Gómez Clinic.'

I walked back to the car through the small park where the girls had been practising their flamenco steps. The younger class had been replaced by girls from the senior school. I leaned against one of the lemon trees and watched them dance. They were about sixteen and stood in a line in their flame-coloured dresses. When the music started they remained very still, then suddenly arched their backs and lifted their arms. It was a dance of seduction and pain.

Ingrid the Warrior

We have become lovers. Ingrid is naked. Her blond hair is heavy. There is a fine mist of sweat on her face. Two gold bracelets circle her wrists. The blades of the fan spin and rattle above our heads. We are in the back room of the cortigo, a country house with stables near the tourist resort of San José in the heart of the natural park, the Cabo de Gata. Ingrid's three Indian sewing machines are laid out on a long table next to the rolls of fabric and the garments she re-designs for Europe and Asia. An archway leads like a colonnade to the shower room. It is supposed to be a workroom but the bed takes up most of the space. It is vast, a bed for warriors. The sheets are soft dense cotton and she tells me they are not just white, they are deep white with no yellow in it and she brought them with her to Spain from Berlin.

The stone fireplace is swept, though a basket of kindling stands near it. A small axe balances on a large, dry log. In winter, someone will use the axe to shatter the circle of time spiralling through it and make a fire but, now, it's forty degrees outside.

I like

— the way she takes off her heavily embroidered belt
— the way she likes her body
— how her bare feet are covered in red dust
— the jewel in her navel which is like a lake, and how my head rests near it, the way the present is more mysterious than

the past, the way she changes position, like a leaf turning in the wind.

From the window which is barred, I glimpse a tall cactus, its six green arms heavy with prickly pears. It reminds me of a time I stood on a stairway waving to someone who was not there, but this memory fades away because I am on my way to somewhere else, to another country perhaps, ruled by Ingrid, whose body is long and hard like an autobahn.

I like
— her strength
— the way she likes my body
— the wine she stole from her boyfriend's sophisticated cellar
— the way her strength frightens me, but I am frightened anyway
— the fig bread on the table by the bed
— the way she says my name in English

The curves of her body are female, but sometimes when she speaks she sounds like Matthew. She says things like 'the size of this room is insane', 'the logs are cedar, don't they smell crazy?' and then she used this peculiar phrase, 'mission creep'.

I asked her what it meant and when she told me, I felt weird because it is a term for war. It was as if she were fighting a battle, but a digression had occurred, something over and beyond the original mission. I thought again of Margaret Mead, her husbands and all the rest of it, and remembered that the rest of it was her female lover, who was another anthropologist. This must have been on my mind when I wrote that quote on the wall.

I did not need to go to Samoa or Tahiti like Margaret Mead to research human sexuality. The only person I have known from infancy to adulthood is myself, but my own sexuality is an enigma to me. Ingrid's body is a naked light bulb. She puts her hand over my mouth but her mouth is open, too. I have seen her face before I met her, once in Hotel Lorca and then in a mirror when the day was slow and now she lifts her back and we change position.

Meeting Ingrid is an assignment that had been scheduled without either of us writing it down. It was there anyway, like a bruise before a fall.

After a while we walked into the shower room. It was tiled from wall to ceiling in squares of flint-coloured stone. The water poured down like a tropical storm, except it was icy and we shuddered as it fell over our breasts.

As we walked out of the shower we both knew something was wrong. It was a feeling of danger. Invisible, but there. Noiseless, but the hairs on our arms were raised. And then we saw it slither out of the basket of kindling by the fire. It was blue, like a streak of lightning as it made its way across the stone floor to the far side of the room near the window.

'A snake.' Ingrid's voice was calm but slightly higher than usual. A white towel was wrapped round her body, her hair dripping wet. She said it again in Spanish: '*Serpiente.*'

She walked towards the small axe that was placed on top of the log. The snake lay very still by the edge of the wall. She crept towards it slowly, holding the axe as if it were a golf club, leaving a trail of her wet footprints on the stone floor. She lifted the axe a few inches and struck hard on the head of the snake. Its severed body curled up and then continued to writhe in two parts.

I was trembling but I knew that I must not shout or show Ingrid my fear. She used the axe to turn the snake over. Its underbelly was white. It was still looping its body. She turned to me, the axe in her hand, the towel draped around her body like a toga, her upper arms muscled and lean from her boxing classes, and she spoke in German: '*Eine Schlange.*'

I told her to move away from it, but she wanted me to come to her. Her fingers which could thread the most delicate needle were still wrapped around the axe and I was frightened, but I had been frightened from the first day I met her. I was not convinced the snake was dead, even though it lay severed in two on the floor. I walked to Matthew's bottle of wine and drank from it, my lips now purple, my tongue rasping. It was like drinking crushed plums and bay leaves, and I walked over to her and kissed her. While my left arm circled her waist, my right arm removed the axe from her fingers.

We dressed as if there weren't a dead snake in the room, put on our dresses and rings and adjusted our earrings, brushed our hair and left the room, the white soft sheets with their hundreds of threads, the sewing machines and fabrics, the thick walls and wooden beams, the fig bread, the bottle of aromatic wine and a blue snake lying in two parts, our wet footprints on the stone floor and the shower still dripping.

As we made our way to the car, I saw a man in tight beige riding breeches leaning his back against the door. He was short and swarthy. Ingrid told me he was the riding teacher, Leonardo, the man who rented her the cortigo. He was smoking a cigarette and looking at her, then his gaze shifted to me.

I moved my hair out of my eyes. I could feel him slipping something to me in his gaze, like a dodgy drug deal in a pub where someone slips a wad of dirty banknotes to someone else. He was threatening me.

He was telling me he did not have a high opinion of what he was looking at, that I was someone who must be cut down to size, to a size he could manage to frighten with his eyes, which were the avatars of his mind.

He was making me weaker.

I had to strike down his gaze, which was his mind, to cut off his head with my gaze, just as Ingrid had, more literally, cut off the head of the snake, so I stared right back and slipped my own gaze into his eyes.

He froze with the cigarette stuck mid-air between his thumb and forefinger.

Ingrid suddenly ran to him and kissed him on the lips. That seemed to wake him up. He high-fived her, *slap*, hand to hand, while Ingrid leaned athletically towards him, his hand still in her hand because they hadn't let go of each other during the high five.

It was as if she were coming in with a sort of betrayal – yes, I might be with her, but I'm not like her, I'm with you.

They started to speak to each other in Spanish while the horses stamped their hooves in the stables nearby.

I'm not sure what it is that Ingrid wants from me. My life is not enviable. Even I don't want it. Yet, despite being on my knees in lack of glamour (my sick mother, my dead-end job), she desires me and wants my attention.

Ingrid was telling Leonardo all about seeing off the snake. He pressed the bicep of her right arm with his bitten-down fingernails as if to say, *My, how strong you are, to see off a snake on your own.*

His brown leather riding boots came up to his knees.

Ingrid looked ecstatic. 'Leonardo says he will give me his boots.'

'Yes,' he said. 'You will need these boots to ride my best Andalusian. His name is Rey, because he is the king of horses, and he has a beautiful mane, like you.'

Ingrid laughed, braiding her hair with her fingers as she leaned in to him.

I turned to Leonardo, and my voice was calm. 'She will ride the Andalusian with a bow and arrow in her hand.'

Ingrid lashed the back of her hand with the ends of her hair. 'Oh, really, Zoffie? Who will I shoot?'

'You will shoot me. You will shoot the arrow of your desire into my heart. In fact, that has already happened.'

She looked startled for a moment and then she clapped her hands over my mouth. 'Zoffie is half Greek,' she said to Leonardo, as if this explained everything.

Leonardo gave her a friendly, soft punch. He would bring round the boots sometime and he would show her how to polish them.

'Gracias, Leonardo.' Her eyes were wide, her cheeks flushed. 'Zoffie is going to drive me home. She is a learner driver.'

Lame

I haven't slept for three nights. The heat. The mosquitos. The medusas in the oily sea. The stripped mountains. The German shepherd I freed who might have drowned. The relentless knocking on the door of the beach house. I have locked it now and don't answer, except for yesterday, when it was Juan. It was his day off and he offered to take me on his moped to Cala San Pedro. It is the only beach with a freshwater spring. He said we could drive half the way on the road, then his friend would take us there by boat. I told him my mother was in a melancholy mood. I am her legs and she is lame. I don't know what to do with myself. I have started to limp again. I have lost the car keys and I can't find my hairbrush.

The incident with the snake and then Leonardo undermining me kept colliding with my other thoughts.

I was frightened when I took the axe from Ingrid's hand. But not frightened enough not to want to know what will happen next.

Leonardo has become her new shield.

My mother was speaking to me but I was not listening, and she could tell because she raised her voice. 'I suppose you had another happy day in the sunshine?'

I told her I did nothing, nothing at all.

'How wonderful to do nothing. Nothing is such a privilege. I have been stripped of my medication and I am waiting for something to happen.'

She glanced at the gangster watch on her wrist. It was still ticking. It told perfect time. She was waiting for something while her watch ticked. It was hard for her to come off all her medication. Waiting for new pain was the big adventure in her life. While she waited she tore off small pieces of soft white bread, rolled them into a ball in the palm of her hand and sucked them for hours. The bread pellets resembled her pills and gave her some comfort. She was waiting. Waiting every day for something that might not appear. A rhyme I had learned in junior school came to mind.

> *As I was going up the stair*
> *I met a man who wasn't there.*
> *He wasn't there again today*
> *I wish, I wish he'd stay away.*

'Whatever you are waiting for may not arrive,' I said. 'It wasn't there yesterday, and it is not here today.' I asked her if she would like something more substantial to eat than bread.

'No. I only eat because I can't take medication on an empty stomach.'

I puzzled over this and then turned away from her and gazed at the shattered screen saver on my laptop.

'I suppose I am boring you, Sofia. Well, I am bored, too. How are you going to entertain me tonight?'

'No. You entertain me.' I was getting bolder.

She adjusted her lips to look even more hard done by than usual. 'Do you think a person in pain with no help is a sort of clown?'

'No, I do not.'

The constellations of my screen saver floated past my eyes, misty, undefined shapes. One of them looked like a calf. Where will it find grass in this galaxy? It will have to eat stars.

Rose prodded my shoulder. 'I told the doctor I have a chronic degenerative condition. He confesses he knows very little about chronic pain. He says this might surprise modern patients, and I am surprised, because what are we paying him to do? He said my pain has not yet yielded up its secrets. All I know is that my pain magnifies every day.'

'Do your feet hurt?'

'No, they are numb.'

'So what kind of pain magnifies every day?'

She shut her eyes. She opened her eyes. 'You could help me. You could go to the *farmacia* and buy me my painkillers, Sofia. You don't need a prescription here in Spain.'

When I refused, she told me I was getting plump. She demanded a cup of tea, Yorkshire tea. She was missing the Wolds, which she hadn't seen for twenty years. I brought the tea to her in a mug with 'ELVIS LIVES' written across its side. She grabbed it from me and looked aggrieved, as if I had given her something she had not requested and was forcing her to drink. Was it the 'ELVIS LIVES' that made her do that scowling thing with her lips? Would it cheer her up to remind her that Elvis was actually dead? Grievance. Grief. Grieving. She more or less inhabited a building called Grievance Heights. Is this where I will have to live, too? Is it? Has Rose already put my name down for an apartment in Grievance Heights? What if I can't afford to live anywhere else? I must remove my name from that waiting list, that long queue of forlorn daughters trailing back to the beginning of time.

Rose was sitting in her chair. Her back view was terrible to behold. It was vulnerable. People look more like how they really are from the back. Her hair was pinned up and I could see her neck. Her hair was thinning. There were a few curls on her neck, but it was the cardigan she had neatly draped over her shoulders in the heat of the desert that made me think she had inherited this ritual from her mother and exported it to Almería. It was very touching, that cardigan. My love for my mother is like an axe. It cuts very deep.

'Are you okay?'

For as long as I can remember, it was me asking her that question. If I wasn't asking it out loud, I was asking it in my head: is my mother okay, is she okay? Rose's tone was cross, perhaps a little bewildered, and it occurred to me she might not have asked me because she did not want to hear the answer. Questions and answers are a complex code, as are the structures of kinship.

F = Father. M = Mother. SS = Same sex. OS = Opposite sex. I have no G (Siblings) or C (Children) or H (Husband), nor do I have a Godparent (who we classify as fictive kin because godparents can make up their responsibilities and duties).

I am not okay. Not at all and haven't been for some time.

I did not tell her how discouraged I felt and that I was ashamed I was not more resilient and all the rest of it which included wanting a bigger life but that so far I had not been bold enough to make a bid for the things I wanted to happen and I feared it was written in the stars that I might end up with a reduced life like hers which is why I was searching for the answer to the conversation her lame legs were having with the world but I was also scared there might be something wrong with her spine or that she had a major illness. The word 'major' was in my mind that night in southern Spain. It was 7 p.m., which is twilight, the end of the long day of sunshine and the start of early evening, and with my eyes firmly on the cracked cosmology of shattered lonely stars and milky clouds, I heard a kind of lament slipping from my lips about losing my way, stuff about a lost spaceship and putting my helmet on and how something was wrong and how I had lost contact with Earth but no one could hear me.

I could see Rose shuffling her legs, her left ankle twisting in her slipper, and I was not really sure who it was I was singing to, whether it was M or F or H or G or the fictive Godparent or even Ingrid Bauer. I could smell calamari being fried in the café in the square, but I was missing England, toast and milky tea and rainclouds. I heard my voice was very London because that's where I was born, and then I left the room. My mother was calling to me, she called my name over and over – 'Sofia Sofia Sofia' – and then she shouted, but it was not an angry shout, and I suppose I wanted my ghostly mother to rise from the shattered stars made in China and say *tomorrow is another day, you will land safely you will you will.*

I walked into the kitchen and on the table was the fake ancient Greek vase with the frieze of female slaves carrying jugs of water on their heads. I grabbed it and threw it on the floor. As it crashed and shattered, the venom from the medusa stings made me feel like I was floating in the most peculiar way.

When I looked up, my mother was standing – she was actually standing – in the kitchen among the shards of fake ancient Greece. She was tall. A cardigan was lightly draped over her shoulders. She had worked all her life and she had a driving licence, but she would have been neither a citizen nor a foreigner in ancient Greece. She would have had no rights in these ruins that were once a whole civilization which saw her as a vessel to impregnate. I was the daughter who had thrown the vessel to the floor and smashed it. My mother had tried to keep it together for a while. She taught herself how to make salty goat's cheese for my father I remember I remember, warming the milk, adding the yogurt, stirring in the rennet, cutting the curds, doing something with muslin and brine, pickling cheese in jars. She put herbs on the lamb she roasted for him, herbs she had never heard of in Warter, Yorkshire, but when he left she could not pay the bills with herbs and cheese I remember, I do remember, she had to walk out of the kitchen and do something else, I remember she turned the oven off and put her coat on and she opened the front door and there was a wolf waiting for us on the mat but she chased it away and found a job and her lips were not puckered, her eyelashes were not curled when she sat in the library day after day indexing books, but her hair was always perfect and it was held up with one pin.

'Sofia, what's wrong with you?'

I started to tell her but a children's entertainer in the square was letting off firecrackers. I could hear the children laughing and knew he was on a unicycle, blowing fire out of his mouth. I looked at the broken pieces of the fake Greek vase and reckoned it was a sign to fly to my father in Athens.

Nothing to Declare

My father was waiting for me at Athens International Airport, but he was not alone. I was alone with my suitcase and he was standing in the company of his new wife, who was holding their new baby daughter in her arms. I waved to him and the sound between us was the wheels of my suitcase on the marble floor. We had not seen each other for eleven years but we recognized each other with no hesitation. As I got closer he walked towards me and took my suitcase, then he kissed my cheek and said, 'Welcome.' He was tanned and relaxed. If anything his hair had become blacker, but I remembered it as silver, and he was wearing a blue shirt that had been ironed with care, its creases sharp at the elbow and collar.

'Hello, Christos.'

'Call me Papa.'

I'm not sure I can do that, but if I write it down I'll see what it looks like.

As we made our way towards his new family, Papa asked me about the flight. Had I managed to have a nap and did they serve a snack and did I have a window seat and were the toilets clean, and then we were standing next to his wife and younger daughter.

'This is Alexandra, and this is your sister, Evangeline. Her name means "messenger", like an angel.'

Alexandra had short, straight, black hair and she was wearing spectacles. She was quite plain but young, and her blue denim shirt (made by Levi Strauss) was damp from the milk in her breasts. She was sallow and looked tired. A steel brace was clamped across her front teeth. She peered at me from behind the lenses of her spectacles, and she was open and friendly, a little wary but, most of all, welcoming. I took a look at Evangeline, who also had black hair, lots of it. My sister opened her eyes. They were brown and lustrous, like rain glittering on a roof.

When my father and his new wife gazed down at Evangeline I could see the truest love in their eyes, the sort of love that is naked and without shame.

They were a family. They looked as right together as a 69-year-old man and a 29-year-old woman can possibly look. Mostly they looked wrong, like a father and daughter and grandchild, but as wrong goes, the affection between them was right. My father, Christos Papastergiadis, was caring for two new women. He had made another life, and I was part of the old life that had made him unhappy. To give myself courage I had pinned up my hair with three scarlet flamenco flower hairgrips I had bought in Spain.

He told me he would get the car and we were to wait outside at the pick-up point, then he gave me some information. Apparently, there was a bus – number X95 – parked right outside the airport exit. It cost five euro and I should know the next time I was in Athens that it would take me to Syntagma Square in the centre. Papa jangled the car keys above Evangeline's head like a kindly grandfather and then disappeared through a glass door.

I asked Alexandra if she would like an iced coffee because I was about to buy one at the kiosk. She said no, the caffeine would get into her breast milk and Evangeline would become too excited. She smiled, and her teeth braces made her seem much younger than I am. I wondered if she had given birth wearing braces, but she was asking me what I did for a living, and I told her (sipping my frappuccino through a straw) that I hadn't yet figured what to do with my anthropology degree.

'Well, you should go have a look at the Parthenon. Do you know, it is the most important surviving building of classical Greece?'

I do know, yes.

She asked me again, because I had answered in my mind and not spoken the words out loud.

'The Parthenon,' she repeated.

'I have heard of it, yes.'

'The Parthenon,' she said again.

'It's a temple,' I said.

Alexandra wore slippers made from grey felt with white fluffy felt clouds glued on the toes. The clouds had two button eyes that rolled when she moved her feet. Do clouds have eyes? Sometimes storm clouds are represented as a face with puffed-out cheeks to suggest wind, but they don't usually have rolling eyes. That's because they were not clouds. They were lambs.

Alexandra saw me staring at her feet and she laughed. 'They are comforting. I paid just less than seventy euro for them. Really, they are slippers for inside, but they have sturdy rubber soles so I can wear them outside.'

My father's new bride child wore braces and animal shoes. My eyes started to roam around her, just in case I discovered ladybird earrings or a ring with a smiley face, but all I could see were two small moles on her neck and one just above her lip. I realized that my mother was sophisticated. Lurking behind the partition of her illness was a glamorous woman who knew how to put an outfit together.

The car arrived. Alexandra and Evangeline were helped into the back seat by Papa. I have said 'Papa' out loud and to myself a few times now and I quite like the sound of it. He took a while arranging the seat belt over Alexandra's lap while she held the baby. He unfolded a small white sheet and spread it over her knees and told her in English to catch up on some sleep. He gestured to me to get into the front seat. My suitcase was in the boot and my father was driving us down the motorway towards Athens, all the time looking in the mirror to check on the well-being of his family, smiling at Alexandra to reassure her he was here and not somewhere else.

'Where are you living now, Sofia?'

I told him I slept in the storeroom at the Coffee House during the week and at Rose's on weekends.

'Are you having a good rest in Spain? Do you snooze in the afternoons?'

He often used words like 'nap', 'snooze', 'rest'. I explained that I didn't sleep much. Most nights, I lay awake, thinking about my unfinished Ph.D., and there were other duties, too, mostly to do with my mother, who was sick. I told him I could drive now. He congratulated me, then I explained how I didn't have a licence but that was the next thing to do when I returned to London. When he heard Evangeline make a choking noise he said something to Alexandra in Greek, and she answered him back in Greek, and I didn't understand a word. Papa explained there was a shortage of medicines due to 'the crisis' and they were concerned that Evangeline remained healthy. After a while, Alexandra asked me why I did not speak Greek. My father replied on my behalf in English.

'Well, Sofia does not have much of an ear for languages. And she did not go to Greek school on Wednesdays and Saturdays, because her mother thought she had enough on her plate at English school.'

Actually, I had nothing on my plate at English school. I had soup in a flask and, sometimes, it was a Greek soup made with lentils.

'Alexandra speaks fluent Italian. In fact, she is more Italian than Greek.' My father beeped his horn twice.

I heard a high, childish voice whisper, '*Si, parlo Italiano*,' and I jumped, which made my father swerve the car.

When I turned round to look at Alexandra, she was giggling, her hand clapped over her mouth. 'Were you born in Italy then?' I don't know why I sounded so put out. Perhaps she had punctured my status as the only outsider sitting in the family car, which smelt of vomit and milk.

'I don't know for certain.' She shook her head as if it were a mystery. *Identity is always difficult to guarantee.*

I unpinned the flowers from my hair and let the tangle of curls fall past my shoulders. My lips were still cracking. Like the economies of Europe. Like financial institutions everywhere.

That night, I heard Papa singing to Evangeline in Greek when he put her to bed. My sister will have an ear for the language of her father. She will learn the alphabet with its twenty-four letters in its ancient and modern forms from alpha to omega.

Truest love will be her first language. She will learn to say 'Papa' from an early age and mean it. I have more of an ear for the language of symptoms and side effects, because that is my mother's language. Perhaps it is my mother tongue.

The walls of their apartment in the leafy neighbourhood of Kolonaki are entirely covered with framed Donald Duck posters. Outside their apartment, the walls are graffitied with 'OXI OXI OXI'. Alexandra explained that 'OXI' in Greek means 'no'. I said yes, I know *oxi* means no, but why so many ducks? Apparently they were digitally printed on to panels of plywood and arrived in the post with picture hooks in place for easy hanging. She said they cheered her up, because she had never seen any cartoons when she was a child. She pointed to Donald in a sailor outfit, Donald in a Superman outfit, Donald running away from a crocodile, Donald dressed in a purple wizard's hat, Donald jumping through a hoop in a circus ring.

Alexandra smiled. 'He is a child. He likes to have adventures.'

Is Donald Duck a child or a hormonal teenager or an immature adult? Or is he all of those things at the same time, like I probably am? Does he ever weep? What effect does rain have on his mood? When does he say no and when does he say yes?

My mother has seven Lowry prints hanging on the walls of her home. She likes his scenes of everyday life in the rain of industrial north-west England. Lowry's own mother was ill and depressed, so he looked after her and painted at night while she slept. She and I never talk about that part of his life.

Alexandra asks my father to set the table for supper while she shows me the spare bedroom.

'Don't use the best plates,' she says, but he knows that already. If my mother and Lowry's mother were plates – not the best plates, but not the worst plates either – they would have the name of the place they were made stamped on the back: 'Made in Suffering'.

The plates would be displayed on a shelf as heirlooms to be inherited by their unfortunate children.

My little sister, Evangeline. What will she inherit?

A shipping business.

'Sofia,' my father says. 'I have put your flower hairclips on the table in your room. Alexandra will show you where it is.'

The spare bedroom has no windows. It is stifling. The bed is a hard canvas camping bed. It is a storeroom more than a bedroom, just like my room at the Coffee House. Alexandra shut the door with intense focus so as not to wake Evangeline, making *sshh shhh* sounds, until, finally, when she had conquered its very last squeak, she tiptoed down the corridor in her lamb slippers. I lay down on the bed. Twelve seconds passed. I changed the position of the pillow and the bed collapsed to the floor, tipping over the little bedside table with my scarlet flower hairgrips neatly placed on it. Evangeline woke up and started to cry. I remained on the floor with the table lying across my chest and made cycling movements with my legs to stretch them after the plane journey. The door opened and my father walked in.

'No, Papa,' I said. 'No, do not come into my room without knocking first.'

'Are you hurt, Sofia?'

I lay in silence among the broken furniture and continued to cycle my legs.

The table was set with three of their not-best plates and a jug of water. My father recited a prayer that started with 'The poor shall eat and shall be filled' and then he chanted the rest of the prayer in Greek. After that, he sat in silence while Alexandra ladled pasta on to his plate. Alexandra told me it was an Italian regional dish with anchovies and raisins. She had made it herself because she liked the sweet and salty tastes in one dish. My father did not say a single word after he said the prayer, so she had to speak for him. She asked me where I was staying in Spain and if I'd seen a bullfight and if I liked Spanish food and she enquired about the weather, but no one mentioned the turmoil in Athens or asked about my mother. If Rose is the elephant in the room, I can see that Donald Duck is not going to chase her out. He might take a ride on her back or flick a stone at her head with his catapult, but she is too massive a beast for him to see off with his orange, webbed feet.

My father suddenly spoke. 'I unveiled my shame to our Lord, and he has shown himself to me in all his mercy.' He was looking at his plate but I think he was speaking to me.

The Plot

Things got worse. It turns out that Alexandra is a minor mainstream economist. This was useful, because I have come to Athens to call in a debt my father owes me for never being around. Perhaps in his own mind he has absolved himself by putting all his late paternal energy into my sister, Evangeline.

I think he understands that I am his confused and shabby creditor. I should smarten up, stiffen my jaw, put on a jacket and skirt and walk him into an airless room with strobe lighting and a translator to broker a deal, but my body is still thrumming with kisses and caresses in the hot desert nights. It would be easier for him to have me crash out of his life altogether, yet for some reason he wants me to sign off Alexandra. She is his most valuable collateral. He is proud of her and I can see why. She is attentive to her child and to her husband. This makes him gentle and calm.

But his debts go back a long way. As a result of his first default, my mother has a mortgage on my life.

Here I am in the birthplace of Medusa, who left the scars of her venom and rage on my body. I am sitting on a giant, soft, blue sofa next to Alexandra, who is adjusting her glinting braces. The windows are all closed and the air conditioner is on. Her daughter is sleeping on her breast, the cleaner is mopping the floors, and she is sucking a yellow jellied candy sprinkled with sugar.

Is the sting of being a creditor the sort of power that makes me feel happy? Are creditors happier than debtors?

Actually, I'm not sure what the rules are any more and what I want to achieve. It's a total unknown.

What is money?

Money is a medium of exchange. Jade, oxen, rice, eggs, beads, nails, pigs and amber have all been used for making payments and recording debts and credits. And so have children. I have been traded off for Alexandra and Evangeline, but I am supposed to pretend not to notice.

Pretending not to notice and pretending to forget are my special skills. If I were to pluck out my eyes, it would please my father, but memory is like a bar code. I am the human scanner.

Alexandra has sugar stuck to her lips. 'Sofia, I can tell you are anti-austerity. I am a conservative, so I prefer to take the medicine of reforms. We cannot come off our medication if we want to stay in the eurozone. Your papa has taken most of his money out of the bank and put it in a British bank. We don't know what is going to happen.'

It sounds like she's about to give me a lecture, so I stop her to check out her credentials. I blatantly ask her about her qualifications.

It turns out that she went to school in Rome and to university in Athens. Before she met my father she was research assistant to the former chief economist at somewhere important and then research assistant to the director of economic policy at the World Bank and then research assistant to the vice-president of somewhere less important but still massive.

Alexandra invites me to take one of the jellied candies she keeps in a glass bowl on the table. 'If we do not meet our obligations and miss our payments, our creditors will want the clothes off our backs.' She talked of the economic crisis as a serious illness that is contagious and contaminating. Debt is an epidemic raging through Europe, an outbreak that is infectious and needs a vaccine. It had been her job to monitor the behaviour and movements of this infection.

It is agony listening to her while I suck a jellied candy.

The sun is shining outside.

Sunshine is sexy.

It turns out that before she had Evangeline she was working in a bank in Brussels. The offices closed on Friday so she could fly home to my 'papa'.

This time she unwraps a green jelly candy and pops it into her mouth. 'Sofia, we all have to wake up from this nightmare and take our pills.'

I thought about Gómez deleting the pills on my mother's menu of medication, but I did not discuss this with my new stepmother.

Alexandra peers anxiously at me with her smaller brown eye. 'For some years, it was my job to make sure that finance ministers convinced the markets that everything was under control and to insist that the euro would survive.' She is rubbing my new baby sister's back. Now and again, she sort of sticks out her tongue, which is green from the green jelly. I don't know why she does that. Perhaps it's something to do with her braces.

She's four years older than I am and she's making sure the euro survives.

Alexandra has two spots on her chin. Perhaps my father is lying about her age and Evangeline was the result of a teenage pregnancy. I'm starting to get the impression Alexandra hasn't spoken to anyone apart from Christos Papastergiadis for about a year.

'Don't think that a disorderly exit from the eurozone will not affect America, Sofia.'

Actually, I am thinking about Ingrid, and the night she put honey on my cracked lips and how I felt as if I had been embalmed. I am thinking about lying on the beach with Juan after midnight and how when I bought six bottles of *agua sin gas* at the village Spar I had yearned to buy a particular summer glossy magazine with its free gift of Jackie Kennedy sunglasses which was on sale by the tills. The bug-eyed shades attached to the magazine were an approximate copy, it has to be said, the white frames inlaid with her signature Greek-key detail, but all the same I wanted to tear them out of their wrapping and wear them to stroll among the cacti in my very own Camelot of

Lust with Ingrid and Juan at my side. The word Beloved embroidered into the silk of my sun-top has changed my life more than the word euro. Beloved is like a spotlight in the centre of a stage. I have peered at this circle of light from behind the curtains, but it's never occurred to me that I could be a major player.

I am not sure how much desire I am entitled to possess.

Alexandra's left eye is definitely smaller than her right eye.

'I was talking about the USA, Sofia.'

I have always wanted to visit America. Dan from Denver is my closest friend at the Coffee House. I liked to feel his big energy close to me while I ground the coffee beans and labelled the cakes. I even missed doing star jumps with him in between making the flat whites and listening to him talk about his lack of health insurance all over again. Last time we did the jumps he was wondering if he should work in Saudi Arabia to make fast bucks, but he said he'd have to take Prozac to come to terms with the fact that women couldn't drive there. When I thought about him saying that, it occurred to me for the first time that he might have been flirting with me.

And I am panging for artisan coffee.

The Coffee House storeroom seems quite spacious compared to the spare bedroom here in Athens. Now that Dan is sleeping in my ink-stained bed, did he gaze every morning at the wall with the Margaret Mead quote I had written with the marker pen?

It might be that the Coffee House is a field study that has been under my nose all along.

Alexandra is still talking at length about how stock markets would react to fears that Europe will unravel. After a while, she asks if my mother is missing me.

'I hope not.'

She looks sad when I say that.

'Is your mother missing you, Alexandra?'

'I hope so.'

'Do you have your own office in the bank in Brussels?'

'Yes, and there are three subsidized canteens, and I get a good deal for maternity leave.'

'Can you go on strike?'

'I would have to give notice in writing. Are you anti-capitalist?'

I know she needs her husband's first daughter to be anti-everything, so I do not bother to answer. Alexandra has climbed aboard the big boat with her husband and child and I am on a small dinghy heading in a different direction.

She tells me that she gets a 5 per cent household allowance because she is head of her household.

She is head of her household. I don't even have a home that is not my mother's home.

'Does your mama still love your papa?'

'My father only does things that are to his advantage,' I reply.

She stares at me as if I am crazy. And then she laughs. 'Why would he do things that are not to his advantage?'

A squirrel has jumped from the trees overhanging the balcony and is peering in through the locked window. What does it see? Three generations of my family, I suppose.

Why would my father do anything that was not to his advantage? She had said it so lightly, but her question is like a wind blowing through the calm blue folds of their homely sofa. A wind that has even brought the squirrel from the tree to the window. Do I do things that are not to my advantage? I lean against the soft, blue cotton with my hands behind my head, and stretch out my legs. I am wearing shorts and the yellow silk sun-top Ingrid gave me. Alexandra is trying to read the blue word embroidered above my left breast. She is squinting with her smaller eye and I can see her lips moving as she silently spells out Beloved. She is frowning, as if she can't work out what it means but is too shy to ask me to translate.

She claps her hands and the squirrel runs off.

Alexandra has a career, a rich, devoted husband and a child. She has presumably signed her name on the contract for half a share in a valuable apartment in an affluent neighbourhood and her share of shares in her husband's shipping business. She has faith in a god. Where does that leave me? I am living a vague, temporary life in the equivalent of a shed on the fringe of the village. What has stopped me from building a two-storey house in the centre of the village? Neither a god nor my father is the major plot in my own life. I am anti the major plots.

As soon as I say that to myself, I am not so sure. My father is definitely mapped in the cosmology of my screen saver. He is shattered, but functioning. I do not have a plan B to replace my father. And then I see my mother's blue eyes, small and fierce. They shine out at me in the wreck of her body. They are the brightest stars in the shattered galaxy. She has done things that were not to her advantage and I am chained to her sacrifice, mortified by it. What if she had said, *Sofia, I am starting all over again. You are five now so I am off to Hong Kong, farewell, goodbye. I look forward to tasting the dishes from the hawker stalls in the market. I will start with fish-ball soup made from eels and when we next meet I will enchant you with my traveller's tales. You will be living with your grandmother in Yorkshire while I take advantage of the good hospitals, affordable cost of living and the demand for my skills. Don't forget to button your coat in the winter months and to look out for snowdrops on the Wolds in spring.*

Even at five I was older than the stars made in China on my screen saver.

Why would your father do things that are not to his advantage?

Alexandra is still waiting for an answer. My baby sister is now suckling at her breast. Alexandra winces and taps her daughter's nose while she removes her nipple from her lips. She says she is sucking in the wrong way and that her nipple has split. When Evangeline cries at this momentary separation, Alexandra lets her cry, taking time to organize herself into a more comfortable position. She is not too full of the milk of human kindness to do things that are to her disadvantage. And nor is my father. They are a perfect match and they have faith in a god who makes their world more certain than my own.

If only I believed in something like a god. I remember read-ing about a Christian mystic in the Middle Ages called Julian of Norwich. Julian was a woman who wrote about the motherhood of God – she believed that God was truly a mother and a father. It was an interesting belief, but I can barely cope with my own mother and father.

'Why would my father do anything that was not to his advantage?'

This time, I repeat her question out loud. It is a grey area and I am lost in the grey, nodding and shaking my head at the same time. My head is doing all these movements, tipping my chin down and then up again to indicate yes and then moving my head to the left and the right to indicate no. She smiles, and it occurs to me that the steel across her teeth does not stop there, it probably runs through her whole body. She is literally a woman of steel, but then she lowers her voice and moves closer to me on her soft, blue sofa.

'It is not easy to be with an older man. There is a forty-year gap between us, you know.'

I do know. It is hard to believe. All the same, does she think I am her best friend?

I reach for a jellied candy and unwrap it noisily to drown out her confidences.

'Sixty-nine is early old age, really.' She sticks out her tongue again and adjusts her brace. 'He needs to pee all the time and he's a little deaf now, and he's tired all the time. His memory is a big problem. At the airport, when we came to fetch you, he forgot where he parked the car. I would be grateful if you could take the X95 back to the airport when you leave. When we walk together he cannot keep up with me. He needs a new hip. But he has now got four new teeth. When he goes to bed he takes out his lower plate on the ground floor and puts it in a jar of solution.'

At that moment my father walks in.

'Hello, you two girls. It's nice to see that you're getting along.'

Other Things

On my second day in Athens I offered to walk through the park with my father because that was the route he took to get to work. It was the first time we had been alone together without his wife and new daughter, the human shields he used to defend himself from his sullen, sleepless creditor.

We both know that his absence from my life is not the sort of debt that can be paid back but it is exciting to pretend to negotiate a deal. In this sense, I agreed with the graffiti on a wall near the metro that said 'WHAT NEXT?'

I was staggering through the park in black suede platform sandals, and my father was staggering through the park with the burden of the small portion of guilt that his god had not entirely absolved. We were staggering in silence.

It was a relief when he met a colleague from his shipping business, also on his way to the office. They talked about the proposed increased taxes on shipping and then about the large sum of euro in cash they had both hidden for emergencies.

My father was obliged to introduce me as his earlier daughter, an artefact from the past he had left behind in Britain. As well as the platform sandals, I was wearing shorts and a gold-sequinned crop top. My belly was on display and my hair was piled on top of my head with the three flamenco flower clips. It must have been a shock for my father to discover that his full-breasted adult daughter from London was of sexual interest to his colleague.

'I am Sofia.' I shook his hand.

'I am George.' He held on to my hand.

'I am just here for a few days.' I let him continue to hold my hand.

'I suppose you have to get back to work?' He let go of my hand.

'Sofia is a waitress, for the time being,' my father said in Greek.

I am other things, too.

I have a first-class degree and a master's.

I am pulsating with shifting sexualities.

I am sex on tanned legs in suede platform sandals.

I am urban and educated and currently godless.

I do not resemble an acceptable femininity from my father's point of view. I'm not sure, but I think he thinks that I am not honouring the family. I don't know the details. Papa hasn't been in touch for a while to explain my duties and obligations.

'Sofia wears flamenco flowers from Spain in her hair.' My father looked depressed. 'But she was born in Britain and doesn't speak Greek.'

'I last saw my father when I was fourteen,' I explained to George.

'Her mother is a hypochondriac,' my father said in a brotherly tone to George.

'I've been looking after her since I was five,' I said in a sisterly tone to George.

My father started to speak over me. Although I did not understand much of what he said, it was clear that he did not see me as a credit to him. He told me not to bother coming into the office and said goodbye outside the revolving glass doors.

I spent all day in the anthropology museum, and then I walked to the Acropolis and slept in the shadow of the temple.

I think I might have dreamed about the ancient river that is now buried beneath the asphalt streets and modern buildings, the river Eridanos, which flowed through ancient Athens, coursing north of the Acropolis. I could hear the pull of its current as it flowed to the water fountains where slave women were waiting to fill the jars they balanced on their heads.

That night, the baby on her breast again, Alexandra sat on the soft, blue sofa reading a Jane Austen novel out loud to my father. She was practising her English, which was perfect anyway, and he was correcting her pronunciation. Alexandra was reading from *Mansfield Park*: 'If any one faculty of our nature may be called more wonderful than the rest, I do think it is memory.'

My father nodded.

'Mem-orr-ray,' he said in an exaggerated English accent.

'Memory,' Alexandra repeated.

He shoved an orange jelly and then a yellow jelly into his mouth, and he glanced at me. *Listen to how clever she is. She's cleverer than I am, except for choosing to marry me, of course, but I am not complaining.*

I had forgotten to tell him that memory is the subject of my abandoned doctorate.

They were a stable family making new memories.

Or perhaps an unstable family anchored by their god. They went to church every Sunday. 'God is the Lord and he has revealed himself to me,' my father told me, more than once. I could see that the experience of his god was overwhelming. Various members of their congregation kissed Evangeline when we walked out on the streets together. Their priest wore black robes and sunglasses. His hands were kind when he grasped my hands. This was Papa's last shot at another life, even if his wife did complain about the age difference between them on the sly. When he walked away from his old life, he knew he had to forget it had ever happened. I was the only obstacle in his way.

The Cut

Alexandra and I talk every morning on their soft, blue sofa.

We are eating the sweet cherries that I have bought with my few remaining euro for my new family. Cherries were grown in ancient Greece – Ovid mentions picking them on mountaintops. Some of the juice has spilt over the silk sun-top that Ingrid gave me to soothe my medusa stings.

'What does it mean, Sofia?'

'What does what mean?'

'The word on your top?'

I start to think about how to describe the word Beloved. 'It means to be very loved,' I say. 'A true, great love.'

She looks confused. 'I don't think that's right.'

I wonder if she thinks that being very loved is not right for me.

'The word is more violent than that,' she continues.

'Yes, it is a forceful feeling,' I reply. 'When we call someone beloved, it is a strong feeling.'

Last night I dreamed again of Ingrid.

We are lying on a beach and I put my hand on her breast. We both fall asleep. I am woken by Ingrid shouting, 'LOOK!' She is pointing to the print of my hand. It has left a white tattoo on her skin, where everything is brown. She tells me she will wear the print of my monster claws on her body to frighten her enemies.

Alexandra asks me if I could pick up half a kilo of minced lamb and deliver it to the cook. She will make a moussaka for dinner. 'It's a traditional Greek dish, Sofia.'

I can't remember, but I think my mother used to make it.

I made my way to the meat market and stood near the sheep's heads arranged on the stalls, illuminated by light bulbs attached to long, swinging leads. These were older sheep than the baby lambs on Alexandra's slippers. They had been slaughtered. Blood had been shed and their livers piled on silver trays in the fridges. Ropes of their intestines were hanging on hooks. These lambs were killed without any formal rituals to make their death more bearable to the eaters of meat. Yet when early man went off to hunt, it was a traumatic, dangerous activity. He lived closely with the animals, it was not easy to hear their cries and see the blood fall, and so he made rites and rituals to make the murder easier. The women and children required endless bloodletting to keep them alive.

My mobile started to vibrate in my pocket. It was a message from Matthew in Spain.

Gómez must be stopped.

Your mother had to be rehydrated at his clinic yesterday.

All that quack needs is a drum.

Why has Matthew become involved in my mother's care?

It seems to me that Matthew's phone is his drum, but I'm not sure what kind of message he is trying to convey. Messages communicated on drums used to save people's lives when there were no mobile phones or helicopters, no GPS. Without the messages banged out on the hide of animals stretched across a circle of wood, people would have starved to death or been destroyed by fire or warring tribes.

I perched on a stool near the sheep's heads and called Gómez. He reassured me that Rose was in good health. A rota of various staff were with her every day. Now that her medication had been abandoned, 'her morale was high.' However, she refused to drink water, so she had become dehydrated. I explained how it was impossible to find the right water for Rose and this was a problem, given the climate in southern Spain in the summer months.

'All the same,' I said, gazing at the flies crawling into the gouged eye sockets of the sheep's head, 'if the water is always wrong, it gives her something to hope for. One day it will be right, so she will have to find something else to be always wrong.'

'Perhaps,' Gómez replied. 'But I must inform you that I am no longer clinically interested in the walking problem so much as the water problem.'

It was past midnight and I couldn't sleep because my room has no window or air conditioning. I am missing brown bread and Cheddar cheese and even look forward to the autumn mists rolling over the pear tree in my mother's garden. I made my way to the balcony to take advantage of the cool breeze. I was now working on doing things to my advantage, so I thought I would take my pillow and sheet and sleep in the open air. Obviously Alexandra and my father had got there first. They were sitting side by side on two striped deckchairs like an elderly couple perched on the edge of the shore. She was in her nightdress, he in his pyjamas. I was trapped in the corridor, not wanting to interrupt but desperate not to return to the hot spare room.

I had nowhere to go, as usual, and no money to check into a hotel. Even the cheapest fleapit would have a room with some sort of window, or the most basic air-conditioning device.

I leaned my back against the wall and discreetly watched Christos moonbathing with his bridechild.

A sort of ritual was being peformed.

Alexandra offered him a cigar from a box that was resting on her lap. He took it between his fingers, and she moved towards him with a lighter. She waited while he sucked and exhaled and when the tip was glowing under the night sky she put the lighter back into the box.

It was was perhaps an act of devotion. In the distance, the Parthenon glowed on the hill.

It curves upwards, this sacred temple dedicated to Athena, supreme goddess of war. What must it have been like in the fifth century BC when worshippers gathered to pay tribute to their goddess? Did an older man and a young woman, perhaps a girl, sit side by side under the stars at midnight? Did they share sacrificial meat? Girls were married off from the age of fourteen, and their husbands were often in their thirties. Women were for sex and birth, and for spinning and weaving and lamenting at funerals. It was the women and girls who did all the mourning for the loss of kin. Their voices were higher and had more effect as they wailed and tore at their clothes. The men stood further back while the women did the expressing for them.

My problem is that I want to smoke the cigar and for someone else to light it. I want to blow out smoke. Like a volcano. Like a monster. I want to fume. I do not want to be the girl whose job it is to wail in a high-pitched voice at funerals.

A snake. A star. A cigar.

Those were some of the images and words that Ingrid told me surface in her mind when she embroiders. I walked back to my bedroom and found the silk sun-top lying on my camp bed. I had been wearing it nearly every day. It smelt of coconut ice cream and sweat and the Mediterranean sea. I decided to wash it in the bath and then take a cold shower. Evangeline was murmuring in the room next door, her window wide open so her soft, black hair trembled in the breeze.

I bent over the bath which was now full of soapy water and held the wet silk in my hands. I lifted it closer to my eyes. And then closer still.

I had misread the blue word embroidered on the yellow silk.

It was not Beloved.

I had invented a word that was not there.

Beheaded.

It was Beheaded.

To be beloved was my wish, but it was not true.

I lay flat on my back on the cool tiles of the bathroom floor. Ingrid is a seamstress. The needle is her mind. Beheaded is what she was thinking when she was thinking of me and she did not unstitch her thoughts. She gave the word to me, uncensored, inscribed in thread.

Beloved was a hallucination.

The incident with the snake and then Leonardo undermining me kept colliding with other anxious thoughts as I lay on the white tiles. My eyes were wide open while the taps dripped all night long.

History

My sister turns her face in my direction and opens her lustrous, brown eyes. She is lying across her father's knee on the soft, blue sofa. Alexandra rests her head against his shoulder. When he cups her chin in his hand and moves her closer to his lips, I can't help thinking he has seen this exact move in an old film with Clark Gable playing the lead and he's trying it out. Evangeline is beloved by everyone in the room, including me. The word Beloved is like a wound. It hurts. In this sense, Beloved is not so different from Beheaded.

I have a headache, the kind of pain my mother described as a door slamming in her head. I put my hands up to my forehead and trail my fingers down to my eyes, and then I press the tips of my little fingers into my eyelids so everything is black and red and blue.

'Have you got something in your eye, Sofia?'

'Yes. A fly or something. Can I speak to you alone, Papa?'

Alexandra's childish shoes are half slipping off her feet and she's smiling at me, her braces glinting as the sun floods into their living space. That's what it is, a living space, and I am living too intensely in their space. Alexandra now has her arm around my father's shoulder and her fingers are in his hair. He has to disentangle himself from her girlmotherlove to speak to me alone.

We walk to my room, and he closes the door. I'm not sure what I want to say to him, but it's something to do with needing help. I don't know where to begin. So many years have passed in silence between us. Where shall I start? How do we begin a conversation? We would have to move around in time, the past the present and the future, but we are lost in all of them.

We are standing together in the storeroom but we are in a time warp. There is no air in this windowless room, yet the wind is up and we are in a gale. The wind is blowing hard and it is history. I have been lifted into the air, my hair is flying, my arms are stretched out towards him. This force lifts my father, too. His back is slamming against the wall, his arms are flailing.

He wants to cheat history and cheat the storm.

We are standing very still, about a foot away from each other.

I want to tell him that I am anxious about my mother and that I'm not sure I can cope any longer.

I'm wondering if he might be willing to step in.

I don't know what 'stepping in' means. I could ask for financial help. I could ask him to listen while I update him on where we are now. It would take time to do that, and so I suppose I am asking for his time. Is it to his advantage to listen to me speak?

'What is it, Sofia? What do you want to talk about?'

'I am thinking of finishing my doctorate in America.'

He is already far away. He has shut down his eyes and his face has become tight.

'I will need to fund my studies. I will also have to leave Rose alone in Britain. I don't know what to do.'

He shoves his hands into the pockets of his grey trousers. 'Do as you please,' he says. 'There are grants available for overseas study. As for your mother, she has chosen to live as she does. It is not my concern.'

'I am asking for your advice.'

He steps backwards towards the closed door.

'What shall I do, Papa?'

'Please, Sofia. Alexandra needs to sleep because your sister is eating her alive. I need to rest, too.'

Christos. Alexandra. Evangeline.

They all need to nap.

All Greek myths are about unhappy families. I am the part of their family that sleeps on a camp bed in the spare room. Evangeline means 'messenger of good news'. What is my news? I am looking after my father's first wife.

I walk back with him as he makes his way to join his kin on the soft, blue sofa. I am fuming. I stare at the wall to try to become calmer. But the wall is not a clear, cool space, it is full of grinning ducks. My father is furtively looking at me as he folds himself into the sofa with his wife and daughter. He wants me to see his new, happy family from his point of view.

Look at our calm resting!

Listen to the way we do not shout!

Observe the way we all know our place!

Look at how my wife manages our needs!

My view on his family is required to be his view on his family. He would prefer me not to see them from any other point of view.

I do not see things from my father's point of view.

Point of view is becoming my subject.

All my potency is in my head, but my head is not supposed to be the most attractive thing about me. Will my new sister make her father less uncomfortable than I do? She and I have a secret game. Every time I stroke her earlobe, she shuts her eyes. When I tickle the sole of her tiny foot she opens her eyes and gazes at me from her point of view. My father is always keen for them to all shut their eyes.

'Time for some shut-eye' is his favourite sentence.

I left them napping on the soft, blue sofa and walked in the direction of the Acropolis. After a while, I could not continue walking in the heat, so I bought a peach and sat on a bench in the shade. A policeman on a motorbike was chasing a dark-skinned, middle-aged man who was wheeling a supermarket trolley full of scrap metal to trade in at the end of the day. It was not like a high-speed chase in a film, because the man was walking slowly and sometimes he stopped and just stood while the motorbike circled him, but it was still a chase. In the end, he dumped the trolley and walked away. He looked like my teacher at junior school, except he did not have two pens poking out of his shirt pocket.

When I arrived back at the apartment in Kolonaki, Alexandra and Christos were sitting at the table eating white beans in tomato sauce. Alexandra told me they came out of a tin but that my papa had added some dill to the dish. He was partial to dill. I know nothing about him so was pleased to learn he liked dill. That will become a memory. In the future, I would say, yes, my father liked dill, especially on white beans.

Alexandra pointed to a parcel on the table. 'It's from your mother,' she said. It was addressed to Christos Papastergiadis.

Christos was obviously nervous, because he was shovelling the beans into his mouth and pretending the parcel wasn't there.

'Open it, Papa. It's not a severed head or anything.' As soon as I said that, I didn't quite believe it. Maybe the diving-school dog hadn't drowned after all and Rose had cut off its head and sent it by registered post to Athens.

My father picked up a knife and slid it into the brown paper with all its stamps and abundant sticky tape. 'It's something square,' he said. 'It's a box.'

The box had a picture of the Yorkshire Dales on it. Rolling green hills, low stone walls, a stone cottage with a red front door. He turned it over and gazed at the illustration of a tractor parked in a field next to three grazing sheep. 'Teabags. A box of Yorkshire teabags.' And a note. He read it out loud. 'With solidarity in these times of austerity to the family in Kolonaki from the family in East London via our temporary residence in Almería.' Christos glanced at Alexandra.

'He doesn't like tea,' she said.

My father's lips were covered in tomato sauce and dill.

Alexandra passed him a paper napkin. There were several of them neatly folded into a triangle and placed in a glass on the table. 'I always keep napkins on the table because your father likes to make flowers from them. It helps him think.'

I never knew that.

'So,' he said, wiping his mouth on the napkin. 'On your last night, I will take you out for Greek coffee.'

Alexandra was reading the box of Yorkshire teabags, her spectacles perched in her short black hair. 'Sofia, where is Yorkshire?'

'Yorkshire is in northern England. That is where my mother was born. Her maiden name was Booth. Rose Kathleen Booth.' When I said that, I felt like I belonged somewhere that Alexandra did not. To my mother and to her Yorkshire family.

My father threw the napkin down on the table. 'Yorkshire is famous for a beer called bitter.'

On my last day, he took me for the promised Greek coffee in a café called Rosebud. I wondered if this was an unconscious bonding with his first wife. He did after all marry her when she was just a bud, but I didn't feel like asking him in case he started to talk about her thorns. A name like Rose encourages that kind of thing. All the same, it would not be true to say that he was the invisible worm that had destroyed her life. Even I knew that. We sat next to each other and sipped the sweet, muddy coffee from its tiny cup.

'I am very pleased you have met your sister,' he said.

We both watched an old woman begging at various tables. She held a white plastic cup in her hands. She was dignified in her skirt and blouse, her clothes were ironed and darned, a cardigan was draped over her shoulders, just like my mother. Most people dropped a few coins into the cup.

'I am pleased to have met Evangeline, too.'

I noticed that he never smiled. 'To be happy, she must open her heart to our Lord.'

'She will have her own point of view, Papa.'

He waved at some men playing cards nearby. After a while, he told me how much it meant to him that I had gone to the expense of paying for an air ticket to Athens. And of course for driving the hire car all the way from Almería to the airport at Granada.

'Before you leave tomorrow, I would like to give you some spending money.'

I wasn't sure why he wanted to give me spending money the night before I was leaving, but I was touched all the same. He had not given me spending money, as he called it, since I was fourteen, so perhaps that's why it sounded so childish. He took out his wallet, laid it on the table and then prodded the worn, brown leather with his thumb. He seemed surprised when it didn't react.

His two fingers started to search inside it. 'Ah,' he said. 'I forgot to go to the bank.' He dipped his fingers into the wallet again and rummaged around for a long time, finally scooping out a single ten-euro note. He held it up to his eyes. Then he placed it on the table, smoothed it down with the palm of his hand and handed it to me with a flourish.

I finished my coffee and when the woman begging came to my table I slipped the ten-euro note into her plastic cup. She said something in Greek and then she limped nearer to me and kissed my hand. It was the first time anyone had shown me any affection in Athens. It was hard to accept that the first man in my life would do things that were to my disadvantage if they were to his advantage. Yet it was a revelation that somehow set me free.

Christos Papastergiadis seemed to be praying. His eyes were half shut and his lips were moving. At the same time, his fingers hovered above the paper napkins. He pulled the thin tissue out of the stainless-steel box and started to fold it, first in two, then into a square which became a circle, and then, miraculously, a flower with three dense layers of paper petals.

He held it in his hand as if it were an offering, perhaps a votive offering made to gain favour or to be cast into a fountain to make a wish.

I pointed to the flower in his hand and he looked vague, as if he was surprised it was there at all.

I had become bolder. 'I think you have made that flower for me.' At last he looked at me. 'Yes, I have made it for you, Sofia. You like wearing flowers in your hair.' He gave it to me and I thanked him for the thought, which he had not wanted to claim. He was happy to have given me something after all, and even happier that I had not given it away.

I have no plan B to replace my father because I am not sure that I want a husband who is like a father, though I can see this is part of the mix in kinship structures. A wife can be a mother to her husband and a son can be a husband or a mother to his mother and a daughter can be a sister or a mother to her mother who can be a father and a mother to her daughter, which is probably why we are all lurking in each other's sign. It's my bad luck that my father never showed up for me, but I had not changed my surname to Booth, even though it was tempting to have a name that people could spell. He had given me his name and I had not given it away. I had found something to do with it. The name of my father had placed me in a bigger world of names that cannot be easily said or spelt.

That image of him praying at the Rosebud Café was in my mind when we walked back to Kolonaki. I suddenly felt concerned for Alexandra. I had been startled by his disconnection, the way he zoned out when things got difficult between us and how he often spoke out loud to the god who was like a telephone implanted inside his head.

Alexandra was pretending to sleep on the soft, blue sofa when we arrived home. Christos tiptoed towards her, gently took off her slippers with the lambs on the toes and placed them neatly on the floor. He turned off the main light and switched on a lamp, then put his finger to his lips. *Sssssssh.*

'Don't wake her.'

Alexandra was wide awake.

He was always ready at her side with a blanket, a sheet, a cushion. He seemed keen to put her to sleep at every opportunity and she played along with her husband's role as the anaesthetist of their household.

Alexandra was definitely awake. We were looking at each other with our various points of view.

The next morning, I packed my suitcase and folded up the camp bed they had provided for my stay. My father had already left the apartment for work and had not woken me up to say goodbye. I found Alexandra standing in her nightdress on the balcony. She seemed engrossed by the tame squirrel that was leaping across the branches of a tree nearby. She turned Evangeline away from her breast so she could look at it, too.

I think I must have startled her because she jumped when I said goodbye.

'Oh, it is only you, Sofia.'

Who else would it be? If it had been my father, would she have yawned and declared herself ready for a nap on the soft, blue sofa?

When I thanked her for making a space for me in her home, she told me she was sad to see me go because she would have no one to talk to in the mornings.

Her long cotton nightdress was white and virginal, trimmed with lace on the sleeves and neck, unbuttoned so she could feed Evangeline. Today, her short hair was greasy and unbrushed.

I realized that I had never seen her with a friend.

'Do you have brothers and sisters, Alexandra?'

She gazed again at the squirrel. 'Not that I know of.' She told me that she was adopted. She had grown up in Italy but now her parents – not her biological parents – were elderly, so it was not easy for them to make the journey from Rome to Athens to see their granddaughter. She was worried about their pensions because there was austerity in Italy, too, but she had regularly sent them money when she was working. Now it was not so easy to do that because my papa had other plans and ideas, but she thought it would sort itself out in the end.

She turned Evangeline towards her again and kissed her daughter's plump cheeks.

It was almost a holy experience to see the orphaned young mother with her own beloved child clasped to her breast.

Perhaps she had been easy prey for Christos because she longed for a father who was also a husband. The Donald Duck posters and lamb slippers and jellied candies and pretending to sleep on my papa's shoulder might be her attempt to make another childhood for herself. A childhood in which she had not been abandoned.

My sister was clasped to her nipple, her little toes waving in the air as she suckled, her eyes wide open and dazed, oblivious to everything except the dizzying milk in her mother's breast.

Alexandra blinked. 'Would you mind bringing me a glass of water? I haven't got a free hand.'

I filled a glass with water from a bottle in the fridge and put ice in it and a slice of lemon, and then for Alexandra's extra pleasure I threw in a strawberry.

She looked wrung out.

I kissed her pale cheek. 'My sister is lucky to have such a gentle and patient mother.'

She wanted to say something to me but kept swallowing the thought.

'What is it, Alexandra?'

I was getting bolder.

'If you would like me to teach you Greek, I would be happy to have something to do when the baby is sleeping.'

'How will you do that?'

She looked at the squirrel again and pointed out how trusting it was to have come so close. 'Well, if you look at the alphabet while you are in Spain and get familiar with it, then I can email you sentences in Greek and you can reply in Greek, and this way we are having a conversation.'

'Yes, let's give it a go.'

I thanked her again, and then I said in Greek that she should feel more free to help her parents in Rome financially.

It was quite a complicated few sentences to formulate in a language I don't speak, and it was even more complicated because it's she who is the economist.

She smiled and replied in Greek. 'Did you say I should feel "more free"?'

'Yes.'

'I am freer than I have ever been.'

I wanted to ask about this, but I don't have an ear for languages. Anyway, it would take a while for me not to think of the Greek language as the father who walked out on me. I kissed my little sister on the soles of each of her brown feet and then I kissed her hands.

As I wheeled my suitcase to the bus station to catch the X95 to the airport, I suddenly felt more like myself.

Alone.

Lying on top of my clothes in the suitcase was the flower my father had made from his struggling thoughts. A flower made with paper, like the books that my librarian mother had spent her life indexing. She had catalogued over a billion words but she could not find words for how her own wishes for herself had been dispersed in the winds and storms of a world not arranged to her advantage.

The Greek girl is on her way back to Spain. Back to the medusas. The sweaty nights. The dusty alleys. Back to Almería's massive heat. Back to me. I will invite her to plant my olive trees. Her job will be to dig a planting hole. Afterwards, I will have to tie the trees to bamboo poles so the wind will not determine their shape. A tree cannot be given form by the vagaries of the wind.

Medication

My mother started to shout in Spanish for water. *'Agua agua agua agua.'*

It sounded like *agony agony agony.*

It was like being in the same room with Janis Joplin, but without the talent. I brought her a glass of water and then I dipped my finger in the water and spread it over her lips.

'How was your father?'

'He is happy.'

'Was he pleased to see you?'

'I don't know.'

'I'm sorry he was not more welcoming.'

'It's not for you to be his sorry.'

'That's a funny way of putting it.'

'He is his own sorry.'

'I feel for you.'

'You can't do that either. You can't feel for me.'

'You're in an odd mood, Sofia.'

She told me that while I was away she had suffered from water on the knee. Matthew had kindly offered to drive her to the General Hospital in Almería. She had strained a ligament, but it was all straightforward. The doctor had given her a whole new menu of medication. She was feeling nauseous on the antidepressants, although she said it might be the new prescription for high cholesterol and blood pressure, against dizziness and for acid reflux. He had also sorted her out with prescriptions for an anti-diabetic agent, anti-gout, anti-inflammatories, a sleep aid, a muscle relaxant and laxatives, due to the side effects.

I asked her what Gómez thought of her new regime from the hospital.

'He has forbidden me to drive the car.'

'You enjoyed driving the car.'

'I'm enjoying this massage more. You have good hands. If only you could cut your hands off and leave them with me while you go to the beach all day.'

I waited for Pablo's dog to howl, but then I remembered I had freed him.

Big Sea Animal

'You are my inspiration and monster!'

Ingrid and I are lying on the rocks in the shadow of the caves cut into the cliffs above us. We have wrapped big handfuls of black seaweed in our towels to make pillows. My eyelids are dusted with blue glitter, and I'm wearing the white satin halter-neck dress that Ingrid had rescued from the vintage-shop bargain box. It is stained around the hem, so she reckons it's too much like hard work to do anything commercial with it. This time she's embroidered a pattern of geometric blue circles and green lines around the neck. She says it is not abstract because these are the exact markings on the lizard she was trying to hunt before I stood in her way.

I like the way the satin rests on my hips and slips like a wave between my thighs. My hair is starting to go lighter at the ends and I haven't brushed it for almost a week. This morning, Ingrid rubbed coconut oil into my curls and on my shins and feet and on my cracked lips.

'Move closer, Zoffie.'

I move closer. Now her lips are pressed to my ear on our seaweed pillows.

'You are a blue planet with your scary, dark eyes like small animals.'

I have decided to accept the mistake I'd made when I misread the word Beheaded. It is not for me to censor how she thinks with her sewing needle, even if her thoughts hurt me.

'Zoffie, why do you burn those citronella coils at night?'

'How do you know that's what I do?'

'Because I can smell it on you.'

'Mosquitos don't like it,' I say. 'But it makes me feel calm.'

'Are you anxious, then, Zoffie?'

'Yes. I suppose I am.'

'That's what I like about you.'

Ingrid is slapping her arms because there are horseflies on this particular beach. She usually avoids coming here but has made an exception for me. She tells me about Ingmar, who is doing good business since Pablo's deranged dog drowned.

'Don't worry, Zoffie, you gave him the freedom to die.'

'No No No' (whispered in her ear).

'You did him a favour. He was already dead when he was chained. It was not a life.'

'He was not dead. He wanted to change his life.'

'Animals do not have imagination, Zoffie.' (Her hand rests on my stomach.)

'He might not have drowned.'

'Have you seen him anywhere?'

'No.'

'Have you heard him howling recently?'

'No.'

'Shall I change the subject and tell you more about Ingmar?'

'Yes.'

She lies on her hip, facing me in her pale blue fringed bikini. Every now and again she flicks the jewel that pierces her belly button. 'Are you ready, Zoffie?'

'Yes.'

'While you were in Athens, the sea police arrived on a special motorboat on our local beach. They were testing the water and concluded there had been a gasoline spill. So they ordered everyone out of the water. Ingmar got annoyed because all the noise was disturbing his customers. He ran out of his tent in his shorts and told the sea police they were wrong, their machines were not accurate, the sea was clear and it was clean. They got annoyed and ordered him to taste the water. So he scooped an empty water bottle into the sea and drank the whole lot and then he agreed that, yes, there had been a gasoline spill. Now he is sick and can't work and he wants to sue the sea police for forcing him to taste the water.'

'It might be the corpse of Pablo's dog.'

'Definitely, Zoffie! That's what it is! Pablo's drowned dog has contaminated the water.'

The sun beats down on her long, golden body.

'So you ran away from me and went to visit your father?'

'I didn't run away from you.'

'Tell me about your baby sister.'

I describe Evangeline's soft, dark hair, her olive skin and pierced ears. 'Does she look like you?'

'Yes, we have the same eyes. But she will speak three languages. Greek, Italian, English.'

Ingrid lies down on her back again and stares at the sky. 'Shall I tell you about why I am a big, bad sister?'

'Yes.'

She puts her straw hat over her face and starts to talk under the hat so I have to move on to my side and lean on my elbow to hear her. She is speaking in a dull, flat voice, and I have to strain to hear what she is saying.

There had been an accident. When her sister was three and she was five she had pushed her on a swing in the garden and she pushed too hard, not knowing her strength. Her sister had fallen out of the swing. It was a bad accident. She had broken her arm and cracked three ribs. Ingrid stops talking.

'You were only five. You were a child,' I say.

'But I was pushing her too high. She was screaming. She wanted to come down, but I kept on pushing.'

I pick up a white feather lying on the rock and run my finger along its edge.

'Something else happened,' Ingrid says.

I feel the panic I always feel when I'm with Ingrid start to rise in my chest.

'My sister fell on her head. When they X-rayed her skull, they found it had cracked and that her brain was damaged.'

While she speaks, I realize I am holding my breath. My fingers are tearing at the feather.

Ingrid stands up and her hat falls to the ground. She grabs hold of the fishing net she has brought to the beach and walks across the rocks towards the smaller bay hidden round the corner from the main beach. I can see she wants to be alone, so I pick up her hat and place it on her seaweed pillow.

Someone is calling my name.

Julieta Gómez waves to me from the shade of one of the caves. Her hair is wet so she obviously has just been swimming. She is drinking from a bottle of water, tilting it up and taking small sips. When she waves the bottle at me she seems to be inviting me to join her.

I climb across the rocks, tucking the white satin dress into my bikini to free my legs, and sit by her side.

'It's my day off,' she says.

I gaze at Ingrid who is leaning miserably against a rock in the shallows. Now and again she scoops up medusas with her fishing net.

Julieta's teeth are even whiter in the sunshine, her eyelashes long and silky.

She offers me the bottle, but I shake my head. And then I change my mind. The water is cold and calming. The panic I felt when Ingrid told me about her baby sister is still alive in my body like the invisible insects that vibrate in trees at night.

'You look like a pop star, Sofia,' says Julieta. 'All you need is a guitar and a band. My father will play the drums.'

She laughs so loudly that I manage to sort of smile, but my attention is on Ingrid in the shallow bay. She has her back to me. She looks forlorn and alone.

Julieta tells me that one of the paramedics at the clinic dropped her off on his motorbike and will pick her up at the end of the day. Her father was overprotective and instructed his staff to check she was wearing a helmet on the motorbike. He made her mad.

She gestures to her bottle of water. 'I prefer to drink vodka, because it inflames my father. He hates all drugs. He still mourns for my mother, and so he is offended by the idea that medication can dissolve the pain of his memories and reminiscences.'

Ingrid is still scooping up jellyfish in her yellow net and turning them out on the sand.

'Medusas,' I say, as if it is important.

'Yes,' Julieta replies.'It is a myth that if you pee on the sting it calms the pain.'

I jump down from Julieta's cave and make my way back to the seaweed pillows. Early that morning, I had driven to a supermarket out of town to find Ingrid the German salami she likes, and lettuce and oranges and grapes. When she climbs back to the rock she tells me it is too hot for her on this ugly unsheltered beach. She glances towards the cave where Julieta is sunbathing and says she wants to go home.

'Don't go, Ingrid.' My voice is horribly begging.

I am still shocked about her brain-damaged sister and want to tell her, again, that it wasn't her fault. She was a child and she made a mistake, but the word Beheaded keeps getting in the way.

Ingrid pushes past me and starts to pack away her things. 'I want to work, Zoffie. I need to sew. All I want to do now is to find the right thread and begin.'

Near us, a six-year-old boy bites into a giant red tomato as if it were a peach. Juice spurts over his chest. He takes another bite and watches me help Ingrid lace her silver Roman sandals up her shins.

'You are so beautiful, Ingrid.'

She is laughing. She is actually laughing at me.

'I can't laze around all day like you. I have things to do.'

Her mobile starts to ring. I know it is Matthew, controlling her, keeping tabs on where she is and that he knows she is with me.

'I'm on the beach, Matty. Can you hear the sea?'

I reach towards her and grab the phone from her hand.

Ingrid is shouting at me to give it back, but I am running with it towards the sea and she is running after me, tripping over the laces of her silver sandals, so she takes them off and throws them on the sand. She catches up with me and tugs at the hem of my satin dress. I hear it rip and at the same time I throw the phone into the sea.

We both watch it float for three seconds with the medusas, pulsating and calm, circling the phone, and then it sinks.

The sea laps round the hem of my torn satin dress.

Ingrid wipes the sand out of her eyes. 'You are obsessed with me,' she says.

I am certainly obsessed with her power to confuse me. To lift me out of all my certainties, even though I know she does not respect me. I am intrigued by the way she is served by the men who worship her beauty as I do, and how she likes to repair rips and tears with her needle as if she were doing some sort of surgery on herself.

Ingrid wades into the sea and grabs my hair with all her strength. 'Go get my phone, you big animal.'

She pushes my head under the warm, murky water. When I struggle, she pushes me down again, this time with her knee against my shoulder. She keeps on pushing, just as she had pushed her sister on the swing. It is as if she is doing it all over again, repeating that childhood accident, except this time it is with me. Someone else is in the water now. I can feel an arm and then two arms circling my waist, trying to lift me up as Ingrid pushes me down. A wave folds over my head and knocks me over. When I find my balance and surface, Julieta Gómez is in the sea treading water by my side, wringing out her long, wet hair. We can both hear a woman screaming. Her high-pitched yelps are coming from the direction of the small bay by the rocks. Ingrid is hopping on the sand, clutching her right foot. She has stepped on the pile of medusas she collected in her net and then turned out on the sand.

It makes me feel less angry, as if somehow I have transferred the toxin of my rage into her foot.

Julieta looks at me, and then she laughs. 'Your boundaries are made from sand, Sofia.'

'Yes,' I say. 'I know that.'

A seagull drifts with us in the waves.

I return to the rocks and begin to pack up my towel. I do not want Ingrid to leave the beach without me. If anything, I find her more compelling now. Memory is my subject. Ingrid was repeating a traumatic memory from the past and playing it out with me because she knows my boundaries are made of sand.

'Zoffie, you are unruly and chaotic, you are in debt and your beach house is untidy. Now you have thrown my phone into the sea. I don't know what to do. I'm going to lose work.'

'Your clients will have to speak to the fish.'

I slip off the drenched satin dress and start to dry my thighs. The small boy is still eating his giant tomato. He gazes at me for a few seconds and then he runs away.

'You have frightened him, Zoffie, because your face is blue. Your eye shadow is dripping down your cheeks and you look like a sea monster.' She has found the salami and is tearing off the rind. 'I don't want to stay here with the horseflies and medusas.' She stuffs the meat into her mouth and glances up at the caves. 'And, anyway, I don't like your friends.'

Julieta waves at me and I wave back.

Ingrid peers at the raised welts on her stung foot. Her silver sandals are floating in the shallow end of the bay but she is too preoccupied with her stings to notice. 'If you come to my house, you can plant the olive trees while I work and then we can go for a walk when it's cooler.'

It is an invitation. It sounds like the sort of plans that lovers make together.

Ingrid squats down on the rock and pees on her stung foot.

'That's a myth,' I said.

'What is a myth?'

That is a big question. It would be true to say that I was probably obsessed with it.

The first thing Ingrid did when we arrived at her summer house was look for her reels of thread and then she tipped the basket of vintage-shop clothes on to the floor. The needle between her fingers was like a weapon, she sewed as if she were attacking the cloth.

'You are so indolent, Zoffie! You are here to plant the olive trees. First you have to dig the planting holes.'

I don't know how to plant a tree. There are so many things I don't know how to do, but I do know how to keep a secret. Matthew and Julieta were on my mind as I gazed at the house Matthew and Ingrid had made together in Spain. One of the things they had made was an exhibition of their kinship structure. They had pinned up photographs on a cork noticeboard to display their respective families. Matthew's mother and father and Ingrid's father and what looked like Matthew's two brothers and Ingrid's brother or cousin. There were no photographs of her sister. She saw me looking for someone who wasn't there while she pierced the cloth with her needle.

'Can she be happy, Zoffie, without a mind?'

'Who?'

'You know who.'

'Do you mean Hannah?'

Ingrid looked startled, as if she had forgotten she had named her sister that night she gave me the silk top with Beheaded embroidered in blue thread. She wanted to forget, but her needle had remembered for her. I am not idle. And I am not an impartial researcher because I have become involved with my informant.

'Is her mind still like a leaf, Zoffie?'

'A leaf is never still.'

'Does she remember?'

'A mind is never still.'

'Sometimes I just want to blow myself up,' Ingrid whispered.

I knelt at her feet and put my arms around her waist.

She reached for my hair and placed a strand between her lips. 'Do you still like me, Zoffie?'

Someone was tapping at the window.

'Everything is dark until you say yes.'

I said nothing. Nothing at all.

'It is still dark, Zoffie. The whole world is dark.' She peered over my head in the direction of the tapping. 'It is Leonardo,' she said, as if the light had suddenly come back again.

I never thought I would be pleased to see Leonardo again, but his arrival had saved me from answering her question. Ingrid limped slightly as she walked past me towards the front door. Her left foot was still smarting from the stings but she paid no attention to them. Stings were only fascinating to her if they were on my body. She seemed lit up by Leonardo's arrival and shouted, 'Bravo!' when she saw he was clasping a pair of brown leather riding boots to his chest. He nodded curtly at me. *Yes, I know you are here. It is unfortunate. You are always here when I am here.*

The wind rattled the windows while Ingrid slipped her feet into the boots. She stuck her thumbs inside the leather and wriggled and pulled while we watched her. The boots came to just under her knees. She straightened her back, pushing her breasts forward, her head held high, while Leonardo rummaged in his leather bag and took out a helmet. She looked mean and victorious, a girl warrior fighting with the men. Who are her enemies? Am I on the list? What is she fighting for?

Leonardo stepped forward like a lustful slave. 'You will need this helmet when you ride my horse.'

He gently placed it over her head, tucking in her two long plaits, his fingers fumbling with the clasp under her chin while she stood steady and silent. And then she kissed him formally on the cheek.

'In return, I would like to give you an olive tree,' she said.

She strode into the garden in her new boots and helmet and returned with a small sapling.

'I have already planted four, Zoffie is going to plant two and the seventh is for you.'

Leonardo obviously felt that he was required to praise it. 'It is healthy,' he said gloomily.

Ingrid opened the fridge and took out two bottles of beer. She gave one to me and then slipped her hands into her back pocket, took out an opener and popped the lid off the other one for Leonardo. He lifted the cold bottle to his lips and took a gulp while I stood untended to, like the tree, my beer unopened. Ingrid had obviously broken through the glass ceiling of Leonardo's approval. I asked her for the opener. She took the bottle from me and cracked off the lid in one clean movement. I was beginning to understand Ingrid Bauer. She was always pushing me to the edge in one way or another. My boundaries were made from sand so she reckoned she could push them over, and I let her. I gave my unspoken consent because I want to know what's going to happen next, even if it's not to my advantage. Am I self-destructive, or pathetically passive, or reckless, or just experimental, or am I a rigorous cultural anthropologist, or am I in love?

There was something about Ingrid Bauer that touched me very deeply. It was to do with the boots and the helmet. They offered her the chance to gallop out of the story she had told herself about being a big, bad sister, but I suspected she was stuck in it. Perhaps she hadn't finished with it yet. I passed her my bottle of beer. She took it from me, crazed with power, loving her boots and helmet and, watched by foolish Leonardo, put it to her lips, downing the whole bottle in one. He shouted, 'Whoooa!' as if he were taming a wild horse, lifted the bottle to his lips and did not stop until he had finished his too. Ingrid turned to me, her slanted green eyes blazing, the eyes she had told me could see better in the dark than in the daylight. 'Leonardo is going to teach me how to ride his Andalusian.'

There was one thing I knew. I was the most important person in the room. Ingrid's mock-flirtation with Leonardo was designed to hide her desire for me.

She was a voyeur.

Of her own desire.

I understood now that Ingrid Bauer did not literally want to behead me. She wanted to behead her desire for me. Her own desire felt monstrous to her.

She had made of me the monster she felt herself to be.

She had been lurking near me for a long time, watching, secretly observing, waiting for me, spookily still, silent. I had heard her voice in my head all summer, I had seen her hiding and heard her breathing. Breathing the fire of her desire.

'Zoffie, Leonardo and I want to schedule our riding lessons.'

I picked up my bag and slung it over my shoulder. Silver leaves of seaweed drifted in the air.

The Severing

'Take off Mrs Papastergiadis's shoes, please.'

Gómez was sitting in his consulting room, staring at his watch. It was 7 a.m. and he seemed irritated to have to attend to my mother so early in the morning. Julieta Gómez slipped off Rose's shoes and passed them to me.

My mother grimaced, the corners of her mouth falling down, her prominent chin lifted upwards as she spoke. 'I have told you, Mr Gómez,' she said, 'there is no need for a further examination.'

Gómez knelt at her feet and started to wiggle her toes. His wrists were covered in soft black hair. 'Do you feel this?'

'Feel what?'

'The pressure of my fingers on your toes.'

'I have no toes.'

'Is that a no?'

'I no longer want these feet.'

'Thank you.' He nodded at Julieta Gómez, who was now taking notes. His silver eyebrows were fierce. Today, he was wearing a starched white coat that matched his stripe of white hair. The stethoscope that was wrapped around his neck made him look more clinical than usual.

'I suppose you will listen to my heart with that contraption at some stage,' Rose said.

'You have told me there is no point, and I believe you.' Gómez turned towards me and folded his arms across his white coat. 'Your mother has filed a complaint in regard to my clinical practice. We therefore have a visit in two days' time from an executive from Los Angeles and a health official from Barcelona. I will require you both to attend it. I believe the gentleman from Los Angeles is a client of Mr Matthew Broadbent. Mr Broadbent has been coaching him how to communicate effectively with investors.'

When I glanced at Julieta, she was engrossed in her notes.

I asked Rose why she had filed a complaint.

She was sitting very straight and had obviously been arranging her hair since five o'clock that morning. It was immaculately pinned in a chignon. 'Because I have complaints to make. I feel very much better now that I have my medication under control.'

'It is very unlikely,' Gómez replied, 'that your new medication will succeed in making you well. Please keep in mind that we are now waiting for the result of the endoscopy.'

I did not know what an endoscopy was and he explained. 'It is a procedure in which the inside of the body – in this case, the throat – is examined by a device called an endoscope. It is a long, flexible tube with a video camera attached to one end of it.'

'Yes,' Rose said, 'it was uncomfortable but it was not painful.'

Gómez nodded to Julieta who was also in a strange mood because she announced that from now on all further consultations would be minuted by herself. When she wheeled Rose towards the door she did not look at me.

'Sofia Irina, stay behind, please.' Gómez gestured to me to sit on the chair opposite his desk.

I sat down and waited while another nurse came in, carrying a silver tray, and placed it on his desk. On it were two croissants and a glass of orange juice.

Gómez thanked the nurse for his breakfast and instructed her to tell the next patient he was running late. 'I want to talk to you about two matters,' he said to me. 'First, we must discuss the gentleman from the pharmaceutical company. I think you would be interested.'

He lifted the glass of orange juice to his lips, changed his mind and put it down again, untouched. 'Our visitor Señor James from LA needs to find effective strategies to expand his market. He has been harassing me for some years. What he does is very fascinating. First, he creates a disease and then he offers a cure.' He pressed his thumb into the white stripe in his hair.

'How does he create a disease?'

'Let me explain.'

He continued making small circles on his head with his thumb, as if he were trying to remove something unpleasant from inside. After a while, he took the stethoscope from around his neck and placed it on his desk.

'Imagine that you, Sofia Irina, are a little introverted. Let us say that you are shy and need to be bolder and to learn how to protect yourself in the everyday of your life. He would like me to call this a social-anxiety disorder. In this way, I can sell you his medication for the disorder he has invented.' His lips parted and suddenly his smile was so wide I could see myself reflected in his gold teeth. 'But you, Sofia Irina, being a warm-blooded anthropologist, and I, being a warm-blooded man of science, must let out minds wander freely across Las Alpujarras. We must not always be a slave to the pharmaceuticals.' Gómez moved the plate of croissants towards me. 'Please help yourself.'

It felt like a bribe. His tone was kindly but he was definitely on edge. He glanced at the computer on his desk. 'You saw your father in Athens?'

'Yes.'

'And so?'

'My father has written me off.'

'Oh. Like a crashed car beyond repair?'

'No.'

'How have you been written off?'

'He is trying to forget I exist.'

'Is he succeeding?'

'He is trying to exist by forgetting.'

'Is forgetting the opposite of memory?'

'No.'

'So you have not been written off?'

'No.'

He was kinder to me than my own father had been. In the one telephone conversation we'd had while I was in Athens, he had insisted that I was Leonardo da Vinci. Apparently da Vinci also wanted to fly back to the father who abandoned him and that's why he became obsessed with flight. As far as I know, the home-made flying machines he had strapped to his body fell apart and threw him to the ground.

My elbow jutted into the glass of orange juice and knocked it over. The impending visit from the pharmaceutical executive had unnerved me too.

Gómez did not appear to notice as the juice dripped on to the floor. He gestured again towards the untouched croissants. He seemed nervous, but I trusted him. I could sense he had paternal feelings for me.

I took a bite of the croissant.

'You have a certain *je ne sais quoi*, Sofia Irina.'

'Really?'

He nodded.

I was now devouring one of the croissants. I had an appetite beyond my status and size. When I'd finished, Gómez asked me if I would like the other one.

I shook my curls at him. 'No, thanks. That would be unhealthy.'

Gómez glanced at his computer and then at me. 'I don't have good news,' he said. 'I cannot treat your mother. I doubt if she will walk again. Her symptoms are spectral like a ghost, they come and go. They have no physiological substance. While you were in Athens, she was talking to me about amputation. In fact, that is her wish. She has asked for surgery.'

I started to laugh. 'She's joking,' I said. 'You don't understand her Yorkshire humour. She's always saying, "Do away with these feet." It's a turn of phrase.'

He shrugged. 'It is perhaps a joke, certainly a threat. But I have already told her there is nothing I can do for her. She is defeated.'

He went on to say it was not in his remit to undo her words or indeed to undo her wish to sever parts of her body. Instead, he intended to reimburse a large portion of his fee. In fact, he had arranged for this sum to be transferred to her bank the next day.

As I was going up the stair
I met a man who wasn't there.
He wasn't there again today
I wish, I wish he'd stay away.

How could Gómez misinterpret my mother's dark humour and then abandon her, as if she meant what she was saying?

She is my mother. Her legs are my legs. Her pains are my pains. I am her only and she is my only. *I wish, I wish, I wish.*

'There is nothing I can do for her,' he said again.

'But she's having you on,' I shouted. 'It's not literally true, it's not real.'

He touched his chin with the tips of his fingers. 'You have some crumbs on your chin,' he said.

'*It's not real!*' I shouted again.

'Yes, it is hard to accept. However, she intends to pursue her desire for amputation with a consultant in London. In fact, she has already made the appointment.' He told me our conversation was over. I should understand that Mrs Papastergiadis was not his only patient.

I was so shocked I could not stand up. Instead, I glared at the vervet crouched in its glass cage. The rage of my gaze would shatter his final home in Gómez's consulting room. I would free him to run into the sea and drown.

Gómez's gold teeth were on full display. 'I think you would like to free our little primate so he can scamper around the room and read my early editions of Baudelaire. But first you must free yourself from that chair and walk to the door.' His new tone was sharp. 'Go for a hike in the mountains. You must be sure not to borrow your mother's limp or step into her shoes.' He pointed to my hands.

I was still holding my mother's shoes which were no longer attached to her feet.

Yesterday the Greek beauty saw three hens tethered by one leg to the same tree at Señora Bedello's. She started to weep. It is anguish. Angst. Four of the chickens have died in the heat. Let her think no one can see her suffering or how she drags her feet with sadness. Love explodes near her like a war but she never admits she started it. She pretends she has no weapons but she likes the smoke. Love is not all she needs even though she has no one to hold her hand under the stars and say god the moon. She wants a job. I have other things to do too.

Paradise

I am lying naked on the Beach of the Dead. Playa de los Muertos. There is a tiny sliver of glass embedded above my left eyebrow. I don't know how it got there. Playa de los Muertos is a nudist beach. There is no shelter for those who wish to be naked. Two slender girls, perhaps seventeen, are swimming naked in the clear, turquoise sea. A ragged, ugly dog swims between them. When they climb out of the water the girls search for sticks that have been washed up on the shore and hammer them like tent pegs into the shiny, white pebbles. When they drape a green sarong over the sticks to make a canopy of shade, the dog crawls under it and they sit with it in the full blaze of the sun. One of the girls takes out a bottle of water and pours it into a bowl for their beast. When she strokes its mangy fur it howls.

The dog is howling.

It is being stroked but it is still howling.

It is howling for nothing.

Life doesn't get better than this and it is still howling.

It is Pablo's dog. The Alsatian. The German shepherd. The diving-school dog. I'd recognize his howl anywhere. Pablo's dog is alive and howling on the Beach of the Dead.

One of the girls takes out a comb and pulls it through her long, wet hair. The rhythmic movement of the comb seems to calm the agitated animal as he laps up water from the bowl. She is combing her hair and he is lapping up water.

The girls turn their attention away from their forlorn beast and lean their backs against his breathing, wet body. They are facing the horizon. A naked man in his late thirties is throwing pebbles into the sea with his young son. When he senses the naked girls are looking at him, he turns away from their beauty and suddenly throws a small rock into the sea. He is displaying his strength to the girls and they are pretending not to notice, but they have noticed him. The man is a father. He is standing with his son and he is forsworn to someone else. Perhaps he has snared a woman as enchanting as these young girls, at ease with their bodies, attending to the tangles in their wet hair. He has already been caught but he wants to be caught again. It is a hunt. The only sort of hunt where the prey wants to be jumped on and mauled by its predators.

The hot rocks. The transparent sea.

The medusas are in abeyance. They have disappeared from the ocean today. Where have they gone? My face is pressed down on the white pebbles. I am naked apart from the glass sliver near my eyebrow. I no longer want to know what anything means.

The heat of the white pebbles warms my belly, the salty sea leaves white streaks on my brown skin. It is paradise, but I am not happy. I am like the dog that used to belong to Pablo. History is the dark magician inside us, tearing at our liver.

There is a whole day to kill on the Beach of the Dead.

Dan from Denver called to say he has given the walls of the storeroom in the Coffee House a new coat of white paint. It is as if his minor refurbishment has now made my room his room. He pointed out that I had left some of my anthropology textbooks under the bed. What did I want him to do with my shoes and winter coat, both of them hanging on a hook behind the door? It was a catastrophe. The storeroom was my place. It might be a modest, temporary place, but it was my home. I had made my mark on the walls when I wrote out the Margaret Mead quote, using the five semicolons (;;;;;) that are also used in a text message to represent a wink.

I used to say to my classes that the ways to get insight are: to study infants; to study animals; to study primitive people; to be psychoanalysed; to have a religious conversion and get over it; to have a psychotic episode and get over it.

That evening I met Matthew, who was carrying a box of clothes from the vintage shop. He told me it was work for Ingrid to take home to Berlin and asked me if I had a message I would like him to give to her. It was as if I was forbidden to speak to her and could do so only through him.

I stood there in the fiercest late-August sun, sweating, freaked out.

What kind of message did I want to give Ingrid?

I let him wait.

'By the way, Sophie, that bottle of wine you and Inge stole from my cellar? It's a mid-range wine, worth about three hundred pounds. So I reckon you should pay half.'

His hands were full because of the box of clothes, so he waggled one of his white espadrilles in my direction for emphasis.

When I laughed I sounded monstrous to my own ears. 'Tell her that Pablo's dog is alive and free. He can swim because he has a sea past.'

'What do you mean, a sea past?'

'Someone must have trained him to swim when he was a puppy.'

'You're so insane, Sophie.'

Matthew walked towards me, struggling with the box, and kissed me on the cheek. I could tell that his body was cleverer than he was because I liked the feeling of him being close to me. I offered my other insane cheek to his insane lips.

It is 11 p.m. and I am naked again, but this time with Juan. Our bodies are shaking. We are lying on a Turkish rug on the floor of the room he has rented while he has his summer job at the injury hut.

'Sofia,' he says, 'I know your age and I know your country of origin. But I don't know anything about your occupation.'

I like how he is not in love with me.

I like how I am not in love with him.

I like the yellow flesh of the two tiny wild pineapples he bought in the market.

He is kissing my shoulder. He knows I am reading an email from Alexandra.

He asks me to read it out loud.

It is written in Greek, so I will have to translate it into English.

Dear Sofia,
Your sister is missing you. A friend said to me that I have two daughters. I corrected her, no I have one, and she said, no you have two. She meant you. I regard you as a sister, but then I remembered it is my daughter who is your sister. Your papa has told me he will leave all our money to the church when he dies. I tell you this as a sister. Although I too have faith, I need to take care of my daughter, who is your sister too. You should know that I lost my job at the bank in Brussels. I am concerned that my two daughters, yes, one of them is you, and his wife, that is me, will be sacrificed to his god and we will lose our investments and our home. This is also to say I hope the health of your real mother is improving and that her legs are getting better.
Kind wishes to you, Sofia
Alexandra

He asks me to read it to him in Greek. 'It is the right language to read that sort of email.' He knows he is touching me somewhere that makes me tremble.

We discuss America. The country that gave a home to Claude Lévi-Strauss the anthropologist and to Levi Strauss & Co., the manufacturer of blue jeans, and which might also give me a temporary home to finish my doctorate. If its theme is memory, Juan wonders where will I begin and where I will end. While he takes the tiny sliver of glass out of the skin above my eyebrow, I confess that I am often lost in all the dimensions of time, that the past sometimes feels nearer than the present and I often fear the future has already happened.

Restoration

The faux ancient Greek vase I smashed before I left for Athens is still lying in pieces on the table of the beach apartment. I wonder if I should attempt to put it together again. The seven female slaves collecting water by the fountain are shattered. Their slave bodies are broken, their heads cracked. I gaze at them for a long time and then decide not to restore them with putty and a paintbrush. Instead, I open a bottle of wine and drink it on the terrace.

'Get me water, Sofia. Water that is not cold.'

I am a female slave and a female wine drinker.

I bring my mother water that has been boiled in the kettle but has not been chilled in the fridge. It is still the wrong sort of water. I am learning that there are more acceptable shades of wrong. I no longer speak to her. The news of her wish for the amputation has shocked me to the core. She has forsaken her right to any kind of conversation with me because she has replaced words with the surgeon's knife. I cannot live with the violence of her intention or her imagination. In fact, I'm not sure what kind of reality I am living in right now. I don't know what is real. In this sense my own feet are not firmly touching the ground. I no longer have a grip. My mother has abdicated, resigned, relinquished, declined, waived, disclaimed everything and she has taken me down with her. My love for her is like an axe. She has grabbed it from me and is threatening to chop off her feet.

It is also true that this threat of hers, the severing of her limbs, has galvanized me. I am discovering that sleep is for happier people. I am awake all night making my application to complete my doctorate in America. I want to be as far away from Rose as possible. Last night I hammered the keyboard and the sentences found their shape on the shattered digital page under the desert stars. I watched the sun rise. It slips backwards and forwards across the sky but it is the Earth that is moving around the sun, tipping, spinning.

I am spinning with it and I am pressing Send.

I dreamed again of the Greek girl. We are lying on a beach and I put my hand on her breast. We both fall asleep. When she wakes up she shouts, LOOK! She is pointing to the print of my hand. It leaves a white tattoo on her skin where everything is brown. She says, I will wear the print of your monster claws on my body to frighten my enemies.

Gómez on Trial

The senior executive from the pharmaceutical company and the health official from Barcelona were seated on hard wooden chairs below the vervet perched in Gómez's consulting room. One was gaunt with close-cut silver hair. His colleague was plumper with flabby cheeks, thinning black hair greased over his scalp and small wet lips.

The gaunt executive fidgeted with a golf ball in his right hand, tapping it with his thumb, sometimes throwing it a few inches in the air then catching it again. Gómez stood in front of his desk and Julieta perched on it, her legs crossed under what looked like a brand-new, white clinician's coat. My mother sat regally in her wheelchair and I was standing by her side.

Gómez gestured towards the two men. 'Please, may I introduce Mr James from Los Angeles.' He pointed to the gaunt, silver-haired man. 'And Señor Covarrubias from Barcelona.'

He waved his hand in my mother's direction. 'This is my patient Mrs Papastergiadis and her daughter, Sofia Irina.'

The plump official smiled flirtatiously at my mother. 'I hope you are comfortable today,' he said.

'It's nice to be out and about,' she replied.

Mr James threw up his golf ball and caught it again.

'So, please. How can I help you?' Gómez's tone was polite but abrupt.

Mr James from Los Angeles leaned forward and attempted to make eye contact with my mother. The first difficulty he had to overcome was pronouncing her surname. He came up with something that was not, strictly speaking, the name of the person he was referring to. 'I believe that you were admitted into the clinic for two nights. Could you tell us more about this?'

'I was dehydrated,' Rose said solemnly.

'Indeed.' Gómez folded his pinstriped arms. 'And then she was hydrated with intravenous saline. This is at the more basic end of what we do here at the Gómez Clinic. You are right to be concerned about hydration. My patient cannot easily swallow water, which means she cannot easily swallow her medication.'

Mr James nodded and turned to Rose. 'But I understand that you have been taken off all medication?'

'I am back on track now. The doctor at the hospital in Almería was concerned, too.'

Julieta took a step forward. 'Good morning, gentlemen.' She glanced at her father.

Gómez nodded, as if some secret message had been transmitted between them. They both seemed preoccupied and on edge.

'The treatment is proceeding,' Julieta said. 'It is in progress. We have work to do. We wish to conclude this meeting as soon as possible and talk to Mrs Papastergiadis alone.'

'The treatment is over,' my mother said. 'It is not proceeding. I have made other medical arrangements for when I return to London.'

Señor Covarrubias flapped his tie. He spoke perfect English and pronounced my mother's surname with ease. He asked her to list her current medication, which she did at length, while Mr James ticked the questionnaire on his clipboard.

When Rose asked him for some information about one of her new pills, Mr James's tone was reassuring, perhaps even excited. He told her in a whisper that the doctor in Almería was a colleague and the prescription he had given her was to help erase negative internal conversations that can be harmful to the patient.

'What sort of conversations?' Rose leaned forward to hear him better.

'Self-blaming or persecutory.' Mr James seemed to suggest there were other examples but the two he had just mentioned were enough to be getting on with.

'It erases those sorts of conversations?'

'Quietens,' he said.

'Quietens,' she repeated.

'I think in English you say "hushes".' Señor Covarrubias seemed keen to get back to his conversation with my mother. His phone was vibrating in his pocket.

'In the first instance,' he said, 'I want to ask if your consultant has at any time presented you with a progress plan in regard to how your treatment is advancing and what has been achieved?'

'I have not seen a progress plan as such,' Rose said.

'Apologies for taking up your time, Mrs Papastergiadis, but I think we have common goals. We want to know if the treatment so far has helped you become more effective in your life.'

Rose considered the question. It seemed to have knocked her off track. She had become pale and her shoulders were trembling. She sat very still, silent and brooding. She lifted her hand and sort of waved her fingers at me. I don't know what she was attempting to convey but it reminded me of the child in the broken house near the airport who had waved her spoon at the car. Perhaps it meant go away.

Or hello. Or help.

'Could you repeat the question?'

Julieta Gómez stepped in. 'You do not have to answer, Rose. It is your choice.'

Rose stared into Julieta's kind, clear eyes. 'Well, I get up in the morning. I get dressed. I do my hair.'

The men in suits ticked something on their questionnaires as she spoke.

'As a child I ran for miles every day. Jumped over hedges and ditches. I could plait grass and make a whistle. But now I'm a poor owd horse.'

Señor Covarrubias looked up from his clipboard. 'Owd?'

'It's an old word for "old",' she explained.

Mr James took over from his colleague. 'We have called this meeting today because we are not convinced you are in safe hands.'

Gómez cleared his throat. 'Please keep in mind, gentlemen, that so far my patient has been tested for evidence of a stroke, spinal-cord injury, nerve compression, nerve entrapment, multiple sclerosis, muscular dystrophy, motor neurone disease and spinal arthritis. We are yet to discuss the results of a recent endoscopy.'

While Mr James listened to Gómez, he was nervously fiddling with the golf ball. He was frowning as if Gómez were speaking a foreign language, which he was, because he was speaking in English in Spain even though Mr James, who was from Southern California, spoke fluent Spanish.

He threw the golf ball up in the air and it bounced against the shelf above his head.

It was the smallest sound of something shattering, not exactly a tinkle so much as a sharp, clean break. It made the executives jump. They turned around to look at the monkey, its small head fringed with white fur, its fierce, alarmed eyebrows, the long tail held high as if it was about to chirp and chitter, *kek kek kek kek*.

'I apologize,' Mr James said. 'I had no idea it was there.'

From where I was standing, it looked as if the electrocuted monkey was levitating above their heads. Its dead, bright eyes gazed at the senior consultants from Europe and North America. They were the new Great White Hunters with their teams of porters, tent attendants, armed guards and gun bearers, enslaving the people and shooting for ivory. The ivory was my mother. Mr James couldn't even pronounce her name, yet she had bartered with him and exchanged her legs for his stimulants. He had won the land.

Señor Covarrubias leaned forward. 'Do you have concerns you would like to share with us, Sofia?'

The only sound in the room was the ticking of Rose's gangster watch, its circle of fake diamonds sparkling on her thin wrist.

'I don't know if my mother is dead or alive,' I said.

Julieta stared at the wall as if she had disowned me.

'Please continue, Sofia. Don't feel you have to use jargon.' Mr James smiled encouragingly.

Rose thumped her hand on the side of her wheelchair. 'Jargon is not a problem for my daughter. She has a first-class degree.'

She turned to me and spoke in Greek. It was a long time since she had done that. My mother had taught me Greek from about the age of three. We rarely spoke it at home, probably to punish my father. I had worked very hard to erase a whole language, yet it would not hush itself. I wanted to cut off its tongue but it had been in conversation with me every day since my father had left the family house. The odd thing was that she was speaking Greek to make a joke that referred to a stereotype about being born in Yorkshire. The only sentence she spoke in English was 'And I don't own a whippet either.'

I smiled and she laughed. When Julieta glanced at us, she looked anguished. Perhaps the rare complicity she observed between mother and daughter had lifted her own lost mother out of her coffin and placed her somewhere in the room with us. Rose and I looked happier than we actually were. I had spoken freely but my mother had stopped my words with a joke. She had banged her fist, insisting I did not have a problem, and she had made it sound like a compliment.

All the same, Mr James seemed confused and dejected. We had veered way off track. There had been a detour, a diversion, a delay. Rose might be in a wheelchair, but she had been strolling through the alphabet, lingering in the lonely spaces between alpha and omega, and she had come up with words like 'owd' and 'whippet'. They did not fit the story he was making with his questionnaire which sat like The Truth on his lap.

He lifted up his hand and held it in front of his mouth while he whispered to Señor Covarrubias, who nodded and then probed his pocket for his phone. I could see he had received seventy-three emails while he had been ticking and circling with his ballpoint.

'The Gómez Clinic has given me hope.' My voice trembled, but I think I meant it.

Gómez swiftly interrupted me and began to speak in Spanish to the senior executives. It was a long conversation. Now and again, Julieta interrupted. Her tone was efficient, even harsh, but I observed that her emotions were running high. Her left hand was touching her throat. When she raised her voice her father shook his finger at her.

The electrocuted vervet gazed at us all.

Mr James stood up. 'It has been a pleasure to meet you,' he said, lowering his silver head in the direction of my mother's lame feet.

Señor Covarrubias kissed Rose's hand. His nose was slightly flattened, as if he had been in a fight.

'Profunda tristeza,' he said in a deep, tired voice. He dipped his plump fingers into his pocket and took out his car keys with new energy, as if he wanted nothing more than to run to his white limousine parked in the grounds of the clinic and break the speed limit to Barcelona.

After they had left Gómez asked me to leave the room. 'I wish to speak to my patient in private,' he said.

Rose shook her bent arthritic finger at her solemn, unsmiling doctor. 'Mr Gómez, your stuffed primate's glass cage shattered very near my daughter's head. She has a small glass splinter near her eyebrow. Please put a cloth over the cage in future.'

As I made my way to the door, I thought I saw the light go out of my mother. At the same time, I saw her beauty come in. Her cheek-bones, her soft skin – she was suddenly vivid, as if she had become herself.

Vanquishing Sofia

All is calm. All is quiet.

The sun is rising.

A black column of smoke is coiling in the sky. There has been an explosion somewhere far away.

I set off on a hike in the mountains as Gómez had advised, surrendering to the harsh landscape, discovering its detail, the perfect form of the small succulents growing between rocks, the lustre of their skin, their geometry and fleshiness. A bottle of water was stashed in my rucksack, headphones clamped over my ears as I listened to an opera, *Akhnaten*, by Philip Glass. I wanted big music like fire to burn away the random terror that was crawling under my skin. Lizards flashed under my trainers as I walked away from the black smoke in the sky and into the arid valley, heading in the direction of what looked like the ruins of an ancient Arabian castle. After about an hour I stopped to rest in their shade and look for a trace of the path that would take me back to the beach.

She was waiting for me in the distance.

Ingrid sat astride the Andalusian in her helmet and boots. High in the dizzying sky an eagle spread its wings and circled the horse. The delirium of the music thundered through my headphones as she galloped towards me. Her upper arms were muscled, her long hair braided, she gripped the horse with her thighs and the sea glittered below the mountains.

At first I was watching passively, as if I were staring out of a train window at the disappearing landscape, but as she got nearer I became aware of how fast she was riding. I knew that Ingrid played her own strength right to the edge. She took risks and made calculations but sometimes it didn't work out. She had beheaded her sister and she was coming to get me too.

I fell to the ground as if I had been shot, lying flat on my stomach with my hands over my head, the blood in my own body pushing and pulsing like a dark river while the sound of hooves pounded in my ears. The sun turned to shade as the horse jumped over me. The heat of its body was fierce and feral as my heartbeat hammered into the warm earth beneath me.

Ingrid had merged with the sky as she sat high on her kingly horse. My headphones and iPod were lying in a tangle between clumps of thistles and the sunbaked stones but the music was still playing. Its swell and might were now a trickle of tinny sound merging with the bigger sound of the Andalusian's high cries and the smaller cries of invisible desert animals.

'Zoffie, why are you lying on the ground like a cowboy?'

She was pulling at the reins. I realized she had stopped at a distance away from me. I had panicked and flung myself on to the dust and thistles but it had been my own hands that had ripped the headphones off my head.

'Did you really think I was going to run you over with my horse?'

I looked up into the ancient, black, glassy eyes of the Andalusian while Ingrid shouted above it, 'Do you think I am a murderer, Zoffie?'

It is true that I believed she would break my bones with Leonardo's horse.

I must have skinned my knees when I fell to the ground because when I eventually stood up my jeans were ripped.

I limped across the thistles and stones towards the horse.

'Have you written me off, Zoffie?'

'No.'

'Then give me your shirt.'

Standing on tiptoes, I lifted my sweat-soaked shirt over my head and placed it in Ingrid's outstretched hand.

The sun lashed my shoulders.

'Why do you want my shirt?'

She held on to my hand and pulled me closer. 'I gave you a gift, but you gave me nothing back in return. It's hard to embroider silk. It's not easy. It slips away. I sewed your name with a thread called August Blue.' She was still gripping my hand while she worked the reins, as if she was nervous that I would slip away, too.

I had broken the rules of exchange. She had given and I had taken, but I had not reciprocated.

A gift like love is never free.

August Blue.

Blue is my fear of failing and falling and feeling and blue is the August sky above us in Almería. Her helmet has slipped over her eyes. Blue are her tears and the struggle to live in all the dimensions between forgetting and remembering.

She let go of my hand and nudged the horse with her knees.

I watched her adjust her helmet and disappear into the dust with my shirt tucked into the saddle. And then I untangled my headphones from the thistles and put them over my ears, took out my bottle of water which was now hot, and drained the lot.

I began the long walk home in the midday sun in my bra and ripped jeans and sweaty trainers, iPod poking out of my back pocket, headphones again clamped to my ears. I felt alive and roaring as I gazed at the sea below me with its medusas floating in the most peculiar way.

As the desert birds cried out above my head, I was not sure Ingrid's forbidden desire for me was a debt I could ever repay with a gift. Not even with the clothes off my back.

I am in love with Ingrid Bauer and she is in love with me.

She is not a safe person to love, but I'm prepared to take the risk.

Yes, some things are getting bigger, other things are getting smaller. Love is getting bigger and more dangerous. Technology is getting smaller, the human body is getting bigger, my low-rise jeans are cutting into my hips which are round and brown and toned from a month of swimming every day but I am still spilling over the waistband of these jeans not made for hips. I am overflowing like coffee leaking from a paper cup. I wonder, shall I make myself smaller? Do I have enough space on Earth to make myself less?

The coil of black smoke had melted into the sky.

By the time I had finally climbed down the mountain path that led to the beach, I had journeyed as far from myself as I have ever been, far, far away from any landmarks I recognized.

I was flesh thirst desire dust blood lips cracking feet blistered knees skinned hips bruised, but I was so happy not to be napping on a sofa under a blanket with an older man by my side and a baby on my lap.

Walking the Walk

As I got nearer to the beach I could see a rowing boat coming back to shore. It was the boat named *Angelita* that had been moored in the garden of the house with the arch of flowering desert jasmine. The muscled fisherman's son had tied a leather necklace around his right bicep as he rowed his haul of two shining silver swordfish to shore. They lay in the boat like warriors, almost three feet long, their swords perhaps another foot. Two of his brothers waded in to help him drag the boat to the beach, but it was still too heavy and they called for help. I dropped my rucksack on the sand and still in my jeans and bra I ran into the sea and stood with them, gripping the rope and heaving the boat to shore. The fisherman's son took out a heavy knife and started to cut off the sword. When it was severed from the blue-eyed, silver fish, he threw it to me like a matador tossing the ear of a bull into the crowd. It fell at my feet and in that moment I remembered my mother's wish to sever her feet with the surgeon's knife.

I waded into the sea up to my belly button, which is the oldest human scar, and discovered I was crying. My mother had finally succeeded in breaking me. I knelt down in the sea, my hands covering my eyes like they did when I wept as a child and imagined that no one could see me. No one at all. I had wanted to be unseen and misunderstood. If anyone had asked, I wouldn't have known where to begin and where to end. After a while, I turned round to gaze at the space between one cliff and the other, and I saw her.

I saw Her.

A 64-year-old woman in a dress with a pattern of sunflowers printed across the skirt was walking along the shore. She held a hat in her left hand. Yes, it was her and she was walking. At first I thought she was a mirage because I had been in the desert sun all day, a hallucination or a vision or a long-held wish. She was oblivious to everyone and she did not see me. I was about to run to her, run to my mother and throw my arms around her, but she looked content with her own company as she walked the length of the beach. She had the resolve of someone who was wrestling with something impossible in her thoughts, reaching for something she could not grasp. The only way not to be seen by her was to get back into the sea. I waded in again and this time I swam far out with my back to her lively legs. When I eventually turned round to face the shore, Rose Papastergiadis was still walking. A woman in early old age in a pretty dress and a hat taking a stroll barefoot in the sand.

She made her way towards the shower on the wooden ramp where tourists wash the sand off their feet. That is what she was doing, too. Showering her feet that were still attached to her body. I stayed in the water until the sun set and when I swam back to shore the medusas were out in full. I kept on swimming in my jeans and this time I saw a crowd of them, a congregation of medusas, and I sliced through them with my arms, my head under water, kicking my way through the Mediterranean. I was stung on my belly and breasts, but it wasn't the worst thing that had ever happened to me. When I got out of the water I searched for my mother's footprints in the sand. There and there. I picked up a stick and drew a rectangle around the first two prints impressed and preserved in Almería, southern Spain. It was a trail of the footprints of Rose Papastergiadis.

Her toes are spread out, her feet are long because she is tall, perhaps over five foot eleven, she is a bi-ped and there is evidence that she walked in a leisurely fashion, These prints were a record of everything that she is; the first daughter in her family to get herself into university; the first to marry a foreigner and cross the cold, grey Channel to the luminous, warm waters of the Aegean; the first to struggle with a new alphabet; the first to give up the god her mother prayed to and birth a daughter who was as dark as she was fair, short as she was tall; the first to bring up a child on her own. There she is, sixty-four years old, showering the sand off her feet. The tide would take away these footprints inscribed in the wet, firm sand before the surgeon could set upon them.

I am afraid of her and afraid for her.

What if she's not joking about amputation? If she really did that, if she severed her feet, how am I to keep her whole and alive? How can I protect her, and how can I protect myself from her? I have been staring at Rose Papastergiadis from the day I was born, taking care to appear less alert than I am.

You are always so far away, Sofia.

No. I am always too close.

I must never look at her defeat with all I know, because I will turn it to stone with my disdain and my sorrow.

The tide was coming in. As I walked along the beach I saw the girl who was always lying in the sand while her sisters buried her legs to make a mermaid's tail. They were replacing her legs with a stump. I walked over to the girl and dug my hands into the sand until I found her wrists, and with all my strength I pulled her out of her sandy grave. Her sisters screamed and ran to their mother who was sitting a few deckchairs away, smoking a cigarette. She threw it to the sand and ran towards me, the heavy gold chain around her neck swaying from right to left as she cursed me. I ran away fast, fast, faster than a lizard flashing through rocks, until I reached the injury hut.

The yellow medusa flag was flying high. Juan told me the district council was worried that tourists would stop coming to the beach. They were busy making a strategy called 'Plan Medusa', advising bathers 'to beware of the stinging menace in the shallows'. He laughed and then bit into a juicy, red apple. 'You know,' he said, walking away from me, 'the infestation of the jellyfish is due to the decline of natural predators such as the turtle and the tuna, changes in global temperature and rainfall.' He was pacing up and down in his sandals. He smelt of the sea. His beard was glossy. He was slim and brown and he was enjoying his crisp, fresh apple. He walked towards me and moved a few strands of hair away from my eyes. His fingers were wet from the juice of the apple. He was saying something to me in Spanish.

'I appear to be softer than you are, and you appear to be harder than I am. Do you think this is true, Sofia?'

Matricide

My mother was sitting in the chair facing the wall in her sunflower dress. Her slippers were back on her feet and the straw hat lay on the floor, as if she had tossed it there in anger.

'Is that you?'

'Yes, it is me.'

I waited for her to tell me the good news.

Her eyes were firmly fixed on the wall.

It is as if her legs are her co-conspirators, always whispering together and plotting. She had put on the slippers to hide her lively feet from me.

'Get me some water, Sofia.'

Agua con gas, agua sin gas. Which shall I choose?

I opened the fridge and laid my cheek against the door. She had betrayed me. In all these years, I had never lost hope for her recovery, but she did not want to give me hope. I poured her a glass of wrong water and wondered if she might have an appetite after her walk. I found a soft banana and mashed it with milk to give her energy to walk again. And again. And again. She took the plate as a perfectly formed female martyr suffering for an unfathomable cause would take it. Eyes lowered. Lips pinched. Limp hands.

She was hungry.

'You are sunburnt and covered in sand,' she said.

'Yes, it was a great day. It was magnificent. What did you do?'

'Nothing. Nothing, as usual. What is there to do?'

'Well, if you're bored you could cut off your feet.' I shook out the sand and seaweed in my knotted, wet hair. 'I've heard about your amputation plan. You remind me of a beggar who breaks a leg so people will give her money.'

After that she turned on me. It was a hymn of violence and she sang it to me like a full-throated, evil nightingale.

My unbrushed hair repulsed her. I had wasted my intelligence. I suffered from an excess of emotion, while she was restrained and stoic.

Her blue eyes were sad and stricken.

I grasped her hand to comfort her. It was papery and numb.

She told me she was afraid to sleep.

She freed her hand and she started to shout. It was as if a match had been carelessly dropped into a pool of petroleum. She was insatiable as she continued to insult everyone and anything that came to her mind. Her breathing quickened, her cheeks were flushed, her voice was high and trembling. What does rage look like? It looks like my mother's lame legs.

When I crept to the bathroom, I could still hear the hate sentences pouring out of her. She was electrocuting me with her words. She was the electric pylon and I was the vervet slumped on the ground, quivering but still breathing. I showered and felt the medusa stings throb under the warm water. They were inciting me to do something monstrous but I wasn't yet sure what this might be. Sunstroked, blistered and bruised, I was preparing for it. I combed my hair and lined my eyelids with an extra flick at the sides. I was not too sure what I was getting dressed up for, but I knew it was for something big. Ingrid and her horse were still in my mind. She had given me an idea that had probably always lurked inside me anyway. I could hear Rose shouting for more milk to be mixed into her banana.

'Of course.'

I walked into the living room, gently took the plate from her lying, cheating hand (but not as attacking as her lips) and poured more milk into the mixture. This time, I added honey. 'Let me take you out for a drive, at least,' I said.

To my surprise, she agreed. 'Where shall we go?'

'We'll take the route towards Rodalquilar.'

'Very good. I haven't been out all day.' She was ravenous after her walk and spooned the banana mixture through her thin lips with new appetite.

It was a long haul to push her wheelchair to the car. It was Saturday night and the village was crowded with families and their children. I suppose she and I are a family. All the heavy lifting felt like nothing to me. I could have lifted the chair above my head with my new monster fury. My mother had chosen to keep her daughter in her place, forever suspended between hope and despair.

When she was eventually seated in the Berlingo and I was puzzling over the gear called neutral, she told me she couldn't be bothered to put on her seat belt.

'I'll take that as a vote of confidence.'

'Are you expecting someone to turn up in Rodalquilar, Sofia?'

'Not that I know of.'

I took the rough road to cut across the mountains before we joined the motorway. The night was warm. She opened her window to peer at the darkening sky. There were ruins with FOR SALE signs on rusty poles poked into the hard earth. Near the ruins, someone had made a garden. A tall, flowering cactus had toppled over from the weight of its fruit, an abundance of yellow prickly pears. The road was a hazard of holes and small rocks, spraying dust over the windscreen.

I was driving fast and blind by the time I turned left on to the new motorway.

'Water, Sofia, I need water.'

I pulled into a service station and ran into the shop to buy a bottle of water for Rose. A pile of porn films lay on the counter with an assortment of key rings, a solitary bottle of rough country wine and a clay pig moneybox.

By the time we were on the road again the clock on the hire car was positioned at 8.05, the temperature at 25C, my speed 120kph. A decaying Ferris wheel stood abandoned in the desert like an open mouth, a last, cheap laugh.

I stopped the car on the hard shoulder. 'Let's have a look at the sunset,' I said.

There was no sunset to look at but Rose did not seem to notice.

Out came the wheelchair and fifteen minutes of heavy lifting. Rose leaned on my arm and then on my shoulder as she lowered herself into it.

'What are you waiting for, Sofia?'

'I'm just getting my breath back.'

A white lorry was making its way towards us in the distance. It was loaded with tomatoes grown under plastic on the sweltering desert slave farms.

I wheeled my mother into the middle of the road and I left her there.

The Dome

At night the marble dome of the Gómez Clinic resembled a spectral, solitary breast illuminated by the lights hidden in the surrounding succulents. A maternal lighthouse perched on the mountain, its veined, milky marble thrusting out of the purple sea lavender. A nocturnal breast, serene but sinister under the bright night stars. If it was a lighthouse, what did it signal to me, panicking in the desert, all my body shaking? A lighthouse is supposed to help us navigate away from hazards, to steer us into safe harbours. And yet it had seemed to me that for much of my life it had been my mother who was the hazard.

The glass doors of the dome opened soundlessly as I stepped into this marble tomb, not understanding why I was here or what I hoped to find. A young male doctor leaned against a pillar with his back to me while he prodded his phone. The lighting was dim like twilight. I made my way to Gómez's consulting room with no idea if he would be there or what to do if he was, but there was no other place for me to go. I knocked on the oak-panelled door. The noise of my knuckles on the wood made a deep, resonant sound, in contrast to the marble, on which anything that was dropped would shatter. There was no answer so I pushed the heavy door with my shoulder and it opened. It was dark in the room. The computer was switched off, the blinds were down and Gómez's chair was empty. Yet I could sense someone was there. The room smelt odd, like liver or blood, a dark, visceral smell. I looked down at the floor. Gómez was lying on his stomach in the far corner of the room, peering into a cardboard box. I could see the soles of his shoes and his spectacles, which were perched on top of his silver hair. He turned his head to see who was there and looked startled to see it was me. He put his finger to his lips and beckoned me to walk further into the room. I tiptoed towards the box and knelt down next to him. Jodo had birthed her kittens. Three tiny, wet, wrinkled creatures were suckling their mother. She lay outstretched on her side, now and again licking dried blood off their fur.

Gómez moved closer to my ear. 'You see how their eyes are closed? They can smell her, though they cannot yet see her. Each has his favorite teat. The strongest, this white one here, is kneading his paws against his mama to stimulate the flow of her milk.'

Jodo looked anxiously at Gómez as he lightly stroked the fur between her ears with his finger.

'She's licking this one here to keep him warm. See how he is the weakest of the litter? When she licks the weakling she puts her scent on him.'

I told him I had to speak to him urgently. Right now.

He shook his head. 'This is not the right time. You have to have an appointment, Sofia. And you are talking too loudly and scaring my animals.'

I started to sob. 'I think I have killed my mother.'

He had been stroking Jodo. Now, his finger paused. 'And how have you done that?'

'I left her in the road. She can't walk.'

His finger resumed stroking the white fur.

'How do you know she can't walk?'

'She can. But she can't.'

'What does that mean?'

'She can't walk fast.'

'How do you know she can't walk fast? She is not old.'

'Not fast enough.'

'But she can walk?'

'I don't know. I don't know.'

'If you left her in the road, then you know she can walk.'

We were whispering over the kittens, which were suckling and pummelling, licking and pushing.

'Your mother will stand up and walk to the side of the road.'

'What if the lorry doesn't stop?'

'What lorry?'

'There was a lorry in the distance.'

'In the distance?'

'Yes. It was getting closer.'

'But it was in the distance?'

'Yes.'

'Then she will walk away from the lorry.'

My tears dripped over the kittens.

Gómez moved me away from the box.

I sat on the floor with my arms around my knees. 'What is wrong with my mother?'

'You are disturbing Jodo.'

He helped me to my feet and walked me briskly out of his consulting room. 'I have refunded your fee. Now I must get on with watering my garden and attending to my animals.' He looked at his watch. 'But my question is this. What is wrong with you?'

'I don't know if my mother is dead or alive.'

'Yes. That is what all the children of mournful mothers fear. They ask themselves this question every day. Why is she dead when she is alive? You have left your mother in the middle of the road. Perhaps she will accept your challenge to save her own life. It is her life. They are her legs. If she wants to live, she will walk out of danger. But you will have to accept her decision.'

It had never occurred to me that she might not want to live.

'Your confusion is wilful,' he said. 'You are finding a home in ignorance. I told you I was no longer interested in the walking problem. Pay attention, please.'

He was the shaman of the village. He would show me the way. 'Run up six flights of stairs before you return home,' he said.

Gómez is useless. He doesn't know anything. Run up six flights of stairs. It's the sort of thing my grandmother used to say when she wanted to get rid of me.

'We have to mourn our dead, but we cannot let them take over our life.'

Those were his last words. He walked back into the consulting room and closed the door. It seemed like a final goodbye. As if he were saying, *Job done*. Gómez had trance-danced into the mind of the afflicted and with his daughter's help put some sort of cure in motion, yet I was not sure if it was my mother's mind or my own that was afflicted.

The Diagnosis

Rose stood by the window of our beach apartment, looking out at the silver sea. The beach was more or less empty. A few teenagers lay barefoot on the sand, laughing under the night stars.

My mother is so tall.

'Good evening, Fia.' Her voice was calm and dangerous.

I sat down and watched her standing up. She towered over me. It was interesting to see my mother vertical. Like something uncoiled. In my strange state of mind, I thought she might be a ghost. That she had died and come back as a new sort of woman. A tall woman with energy and focus, a woman whose attention was not on unwrapping a pill. She told me years ago that I must write Milky Way like this – $\gamma\alpha\lambda\alpha\xi\iota\alpha\varsigma$ $\kappa\upsilon\kappa\lambda o\varsigma$ – and that Aristotle gazed up at the milky circle in Chalcidice, thirty-four miles east of modern-day Thessaloniki, where my father was born. Yet she never spoke about the stars she gazed upon when she was seven years old in the village of Warter in East Yorkshire, four miles from Pocklington. Did she lie on her back in the Yorkshire Wolds among the snowdrops and make big plans for her life?

I think she did. Where is she mapped in the haunted sky?

'Jodo has had her kittens,' I said.

'How many?'

'Three.'

'Ah. I take it the mother is in good health after the birth?'

I noted she had not asked after the babies.

'I'd like a glass of water,' I said.

She thought about this. 'Say "please".'

'Please.'

I watched her walk into the kitchen, heard the fridge open, the sound of liquid being poured into a glass. She carried the water towards me.

I had been waiting on her all my life. I was the waitress. Waiting on her and waiting for her. What was I waiting for? Waiting for her to step into her self or step out of her invalid self. Waiting for her to take the voyage out of her gloom, to buy a ticket to a vital life. With an extra ticket for me. Yes, I had been waiting all my life for her to reserve a seat for me.

'Cheers.' I raised my glass.

The door to the concrete terrace on the beach opened of its own accord. A breeze filled the room. A warm desert breeze carrying with it the deep, salt smell of seaweed and hot sand. The waves were crashing on the beach, the table on the terrace had my laptop resting on it, the night stars made in China were open under the real night stars in Spain. All summer, I had been moonwalking in the digital Milky Way. It's calm there. But I am not calm. My mind is like the edge of motorways where foxes eat the owls at night. In the starfields, with their faintly glowing paths running across the screen, I have been making footprints in the dust and glitter of the virtual universe. It never occurred to me that, like the medusa, technology stares back and that its gaze might have petrified me, made me fearful to come down, down to Earth, where all the hard stuff happens, down to the check-out tills and the barcodes and the too many words for profit and the not enough words for pain.

'I went for a walk today,' my mother said. 'I was too overwhelmed to share the good news with you.'

'Yes. You have never shared good news with me.'

'I did not want to raise your hopes.'

'You have never wanted to raise my hopes.'

'Do you want to know about the lorry driver who gave me a lift home?'

'No. I don't want to know anything about him.'

'It was a her. The driver was a her.'

Rose put down her glass of water and walked towards me. 'Give up the driving without a licence, Sofia. It was night, and your lights were not switched on. I was in fear for your life. I can't imagine you as a driver.'

'Yes,' I said, 'but you are a driver. You are head of your household. You need to start doing things that are to your advantage.'

'I will try.'

She sat next to me on the hard, green sofa of our rented apartment without any effort at all. 'I will try to do things that are to my advantage, but in the meanwhile I can imagine you finishing your doctorate in America.'

And what did I imagine for her?

I imagine that she is wearing smart shoes with straps over her ankles. She is pointing to her diamond bling watch, inviting me to walk faster so we will not be late for the cinema. She has booked the tickets. Yes, she has chosen our seats. Walk faster, Sofia, faster (she points to her watch), I don't want to miss the trailers.

'There is something else, Sofia.'

'Gómez has already told me.'

'What did he tell you?'

'That he's refunding the money.'

'Oh,' she said. 'He is a very good doctor. He doesn't have to do that.'

She continued talking. At first I thought she was saying Sophocles. She repeated Sophocles about three times. I realized she was saying 'oesophageal'. Oesophageal.

And then she told me the results of the endoscopy.

A long time passed. Her gangster watch ticking. The waves breaking on the sand.

I rested my head on her shoulder. 'It can't be true, Mum.'

Is it easier to surrender to death than to life?

I turned to look at her.

She held my gaze for a long time. Her eyes were dry.

'You have such a blatant stare,' she said, 'but I have watched you as closely as you have watched me. It's what mothers do. We watch our children. We know our gaze is powerful so we pretend not to look.'

The tide was coming in with all the medusas floating in its turbulence. The tendrils of the jellyfish in limbo, like something cut loose, a placenta, a parachute, a refugee severed from its place of origin.

A Note on the Author

Deborah Levy writes fiction, plays, and poetry. Her work has been staged by the Royal Shakespeare Company, widely broadcast on the BBC, and translated into fourteen languages. She is the author of highly praised novels, including *Swimming Home* (shortlisted for the Man Booker Prize in 2012), *The Unloved*, and *Billy and Girl*, the story collection *Black Vodka*, and the essay *Things I Don't Want to Know*. She lives in London.

Also Available from Deborah Levy

Swimming Home

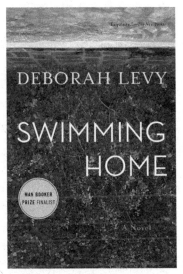

Man Booker Prize Finalist

As he arrives with his family at the villa in the hills above Nice, Joe sees a body in the swimming pool. But the girl is very much alive. She is Kitty Finch: a self-proclaimed botanist with green-painted fingernails, walking naked out of the water and into the heart of their holiday. Why is she there? What does she want from them all? And why does Joe's enigmatic wife allow her to remain?

A subversively brilliant study of love, *Swimming Home* reveals how the most devastating secrets are the ones we keep from ourselves.

"Exquisite." —*The New Yorker*

"Readers will have to resist the temptation to hurry up in order to find out what happens . . . Our reward is the enjoyable, if unsettling, experience of being pitched into the deep waters of Levy's wry, accomplished novel." —Francine Prose, *The New York Times Book Review*

"Here is an excellent story, told with the subtlety and menacing tension of a veteran playwright." —Sam Sacks, *The Wall Street Journal*

"Elegant . . . subtle . . . uncanny . . . The seductive pleasure of Levy's prose stems from its layered brilliance . . . [*Swimming Home* is] witty right up until it's unbearably sad." —Ron Charles, *The Washington Post*

Also Available from Deborah Levy

The Early Novels
Beautiful Mutants, Swallowing Geography, The Unloved

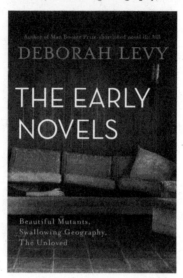

Beautiful Mutants, Deborah Levy's feverish allegory of a first novel, explores the anxieties that pervaded the 1980s: exile and emigration, broken dreams, crazed greed and the first seeds of the global financial crisis, self-destructive desires, and the disintegration of culture.

In *Swallowing Geography*, J.K., like her namesake Jack Kerouac, is always on the road, meeting friends and strangers, battling her raging mother, and taking in the world through her uniquely irreverent, ironic perspective. Levy blends fairytale with biting satire, pushing at the edges of reality and marveling at where the world collapses in on itself.

In *The Unloved*, an international group of hedonistic tourists gathers to celebrate the holidays in a remote French château. Then a woman is brutally murdered, and the subsequent inquiry into her death proves to be more of an investigation into the nature of identity, love, insatiable rage, and sadistic desire.

These early novels illuminate Deborah Levy's development as a novelist, bringing into focus the emergence of her surreal imagination, crystalline prose, and astute, unparalleled insight into the human experience.

"[Levy] writes like a hyperkinetic angel." —*The Times*

"Written during her transition from playwright to prose, Deborah Levy's early works conjure fractured and fluid worlds that are wholly immersive."
—*The Guardian*

Also Available from Deborah Levy

Black Vodka

The stories in *Black Vodka*, by acclaimed author Deborah Levy, are perfectly formed worlds unto themselves, written in elegant yet economical prose. She is a master of the short story, exploring loneliness and belonging; violence and tenderness; the ephemeral and the solid; the grotesque and the beautiful; love and infidelity; and fluid identities national, cultural, and personal. In "Shining a Light," a woman's lost luggage is juxtaposed with far more serious losses; a man's empathy threatens to destroy him in "Stardust Nation"; "Cave Girl" features a girl who wants to be a different kind of woman and succeeds in a shocking way; and a deformed man seeks beauty amid his angst in the title story.

These are twenty-first-century lives dissected with razor-sharp humor and curiosity. Levy's stories will send you tumbling into a rabbit hole, and you won't be able to scramble out until long after you've turned the last page.

"These ominous, odd, erotic stories burrow deep into your brain."
—*Financial Times*

"One of the most exciting voices in contemporary British fiction . . . Sophisticated and astringent." —*The Times Literary Supplement*

Also Available from Deborah Levy

Things I Don't Want to Know

Blending personal history, gender politics, philosophy, and literary theory into a luminescent treatise on writing, love, and loss, *Things I Don't Want to Know* is Deborah Levy's witty response to George Orwell's influential essay "Why I Write." Orwell identified four reasons he was driven to hammer at his typewriter—political purpose, historical impulse, sheer egoism, and aesthetic enthusiasm—and Levy's newest work riffs on these same commitments from a female writer's perspective.

As she struggles to balance womanhood, motherhood, and her writing career, Levy identifies some of the real-life experiences that have shaped her novels, including her family's emigration from South Africa in the era of apartheid; her teenage years in the UK where she played at being a writer in the company of builders and bus drivers in cheap diners; and her theater-writing days touring Poland in the midst of Eastern Europe's economic crisis, where she observed how a soldier tenderly kissed the women in his life good-bye.

Spanning continents (Africa and Europe) and decades (we meet the author at seven, fifteen, and fifty), *Things I Don't Want to Know* brings the reader into a writer's heart.

"A profound and vivid little volume that is less about the craft than the necessity of making literature." —*Los Angeles Times*

"A lively, vivid account of how the most innocent details of a writer's personal story can gain power in fiction." —*The New York Times Book Review*